WHAT DID YOU GIFT YOUR PARENTS TODAY?

DEDICATED TO ALL SONS AND DAUGHTERS LIVING ALIVE

VEERKUMAR SONDUR

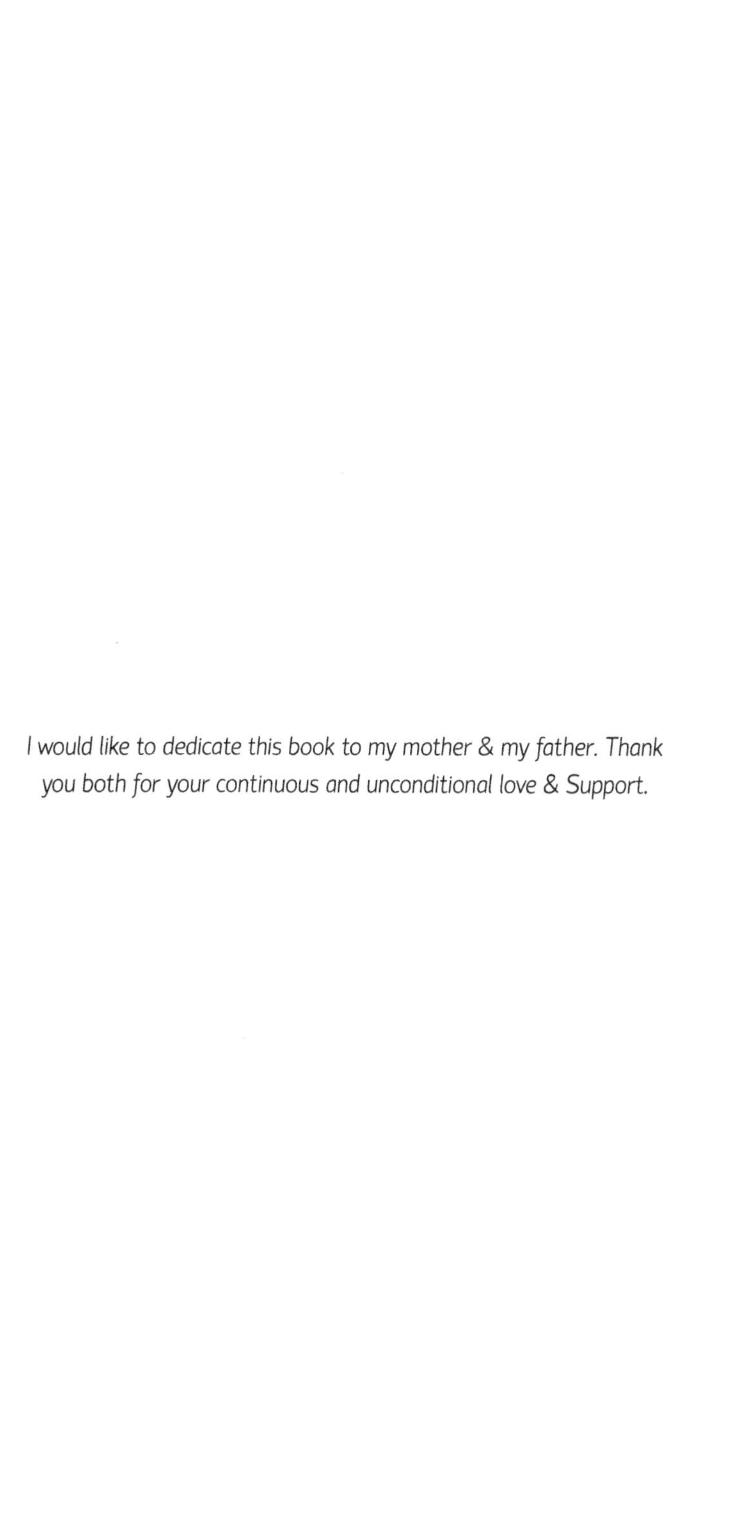

I would like to dedicate this book to my mother & my father. Thank you both for your continuous and unconditional love & Support.

Contents

Foreword

Veerkumar Sondur writer and a poet originally from Shivamogga, Karnataka, India. He has a bachelor's in business management [BBM]from Kuvempu University and an MCA [master's in computer applications] in Computer Science from Visvesvaraya Technological University. After starting in software engineering, he embarked upon a career as a software engineer, writer, and poet. In 2003, Veerkumar was appointed as a software engineer in MNC in Bengaluru. He currently resides in Bengaluru, India, along with his family.

After seeing the life, relations, and society closely for 40+ years, observing the relationship between parents and children, noticing the differences among younger generation and their parents, and spotting the gap amid parents and grownup sons/daughters, felt that the fundamental values of parent-child relationship is getting destroyed slowly. Hence this sacred relationship is at risk. Therefore, coming up with this book to reinstate those missing values and sense of responsibility in parents and children relationship.

Our parents start giving us gifts from the first day of our life. Though we don't understand the meaning and its value on that day, they give it, and we receive it. We not only receive gifts from our loved ones, but we also receive gifts from GOD - Donato. The best gift that we ever received from God is "our parents," and the second-best gift that we receive is "our children."

Usually, we receive gifts from our parents and expect more. At the same time, parents also love to give. But our expectation of more from our parents never dies! Few children even go to the extent of getting it by force as if it is their birth right. It's difficult to satisfy the own blood. Own blood never gets easily satisfied.

Though we receive innumerable gifts from our parents, we rarely offer them any! But we don't know what is that they would like to receive from us as a gift? Obviously, they expect and prefer the precious one! If so, does it cost you too much? No. Not at all! Don't worry about your money. It does not cost you too much. It is not expensive, but very valuable!

Regardless of whether our parents expect gifts from us or not, whether they want to receive it or not, it is the moral responsibility of every living son and daughter to take care of their parents, offering them the right gift at the right time for their happiness and in their honour. After all, gifts are given to show our love, care, concern, affection, and gratitude.

A giving hand is far more powerful than a head bowing in prayer, and a good small act of kindness is always stronger than a thousand good thoughts in mind. So, let's convert all such good small acts of love and kindness into meaningful gifts and offer them to our parents for their happiness and honour.

Preface

Parents experience excitement, joy, happiness, and fun at the beginning of their parenting, but at the same time, they also go through stress, discomfort, and anxiety. According to the findings, parents have a greater gap in happiness than nonparents. If non-parents are not happy, we all can easily understand why they are not happy. Because they don't have what they want. i.e., Own Children! But consider the situation of parents who have gotten what they want but are still unhappy. Because they have gotten what they want. i.e., Own Children! YES! Many parents are not happy because of their own children. By the way, what about your parents? Are they happy?

There will always be dissimilarities and disagreement between you and them and There will always be dispute between what is right and what is wrong. But be mindful about the language that you use and the tone that you raise while expressing your disagreement. Remember that your children will learn from you and behave the way you behave with your parents. If you don't respect your parents, how others will respect them? and if you don't treat them well, how others will do?

Never make them feel, "Why the hell we give birth to this person?". Never make them think "What was the blunder we did to get this kind of a son or daughter?" and not even once create a situation where they are forced to bow their heads out of shyness and disrespect.

Acknowledgements

First and foremost, praises and thanks to my father Jayalingappa Sondur and mother Indira S.J. for their blessings throughout their life. I am extremely grateful to their love, prayer, care and sacrifices for maintaining, educating and preparing me and my sister. I am very much thankful to my sister Mamatha S.J. And I also express my thanks to my beloved wife Sushma Veerkumar B.L, daughters SwarnaGowri S.V and Sirigowri S.V for their continious love, understanding and motivation.

CHAPTER ONE

RESPECT

The first gift is to promise that **"I respect my parents."** 'Respect' is nothing but a positive feeling or a positive action shown towards someone or something for their valuable qualities. It is an act of honoring or admiring someone for their help, love, care, sacrifice, service, quality, ability, achievement, contribution, and need. Therefore, being a responsible individual, **it's our responsibility to respect all those who demonstrate great qualities.**

A study on 'parenting' makes it clear that not all parents are happy. Of course, parents experience excitement, joy, happiness, and fun at the beginning of their parenting, but at the same time, they also go through stress, discomfort, and anxiety. According to the findings, parents have a greater gap in happiness than nonparents. If non-parents are not happy, we all can easily understand why they are not happy. Because they don't have what they want. i.e., Own Children! But consider the situation of parents who have gotten what they want but are still unhappy. Because they have gotten what they want. i.e., Own Children! YES! Many parents are not happy because of their own children. By the way, what about your parents? Are they happy? [Pause reading the book for a moment. Ponder deeply about this question from the bottom of your heart and think what you can do on this]

Even after knowing the truth that there would be more stress, anxiety, inconvenience, disturbance, discomfort and higher responsibility, your parents decide to give birth to you and they get ready to welcome you into their lives. They know that the decision is being taken at the cost of their peace of mind but at the same time, they also know that you bring them the joy, happiness, motive and purpose in their life. Though it is hard and difficult, they stick to their decision to give birth. Because they give more importance to you than their own comfort, ease, joy, difficulties, challenges and happiness. Respect such thoughts and value their decision. Always demonstrate high regard and pay special respect to your parents.

But the most basic and practical question one may ask is, 'Why should I respect my parents? Is it just because I have been given birth? Before finding the answer to this question, please understand that you have not just been given a birth but also a life. [Think over it. Try to understand the difference between "giving birth" and "giving life." It is not the same or as simple as it sounds.] Be clearly aware of the fact that you have not just been given birth, but you have been well taken care of even after your birth.

Before asking, "Why should I respect my parents?" ask yourself, "Do I respect myself?" Those who don't respect themselves are most likely to disrespect others. Those who lack self-respect simply don't care about anyone else. **So, learn to respect yourself before expecting respect from others.** Respecting ourselves shows our dignity and respecting others shows our culture.

Let's come back to our basic question: "Why should I respect my parents?"

Do I have to respect my parents just because they gave birth to me? YES. This one reason is sufficient for you to respect your parents. Because the greatest thing one can do on this earth is to give birth and take responsibility for nurturing that new life in the right way. But, it's not the only reason; it's just one of the reasons to respect them. There are many more valid and meaningful reasons to respect your parents.

She protects you in her stomach at the cost of her life. She tolerates all the mental disturbances and bodily challenges while pregnant. She goes through inconveniences, problems, and troubles. She endures all the pain and issues, but still holds you tight inside and waits. She waits until you are ready; she waits until you are prepared; she waits until you get enough energy to survive on your own outside; she holds until you are complete and delivers only when you are ready to get delivered. Note that you were not taken care of only in the womb, but very well taken care of even after coming out of it. You were not only protected, saved, and safeguarded inside her stomach but also well looked after outside.

During those 9+ months, her body goes through painful changes and miraculous transformation. Her body goes shapeless; she gains weight, belly swells; leg pains, foot slips, back aches, tired eyes, and a runny nose. Her skin itches. It stretches, sleepless nights, dark circles, short breaths, and body ache. The hormonal change brings up unwanted emotions and unnecessary reactions. Her emotions go up and down, left, and right, all over the places. Anger, fear, love, sadness, joy, and surprises come up easily and go down very often.

Apart from the outer physical challenges and frequent emotional changes, she also undergoes complex transformation within her body. She goes through all the hard times of the pregnancy cycle just for you and only for you. She literally creates a small globe within her stomach just to take care of you! Remember that your mother is the only person after God who can create this one-of-a-kind globe solely for you and only for you. She creates it exclusively for you. and bears its weight all alone. **Mother's love is mother of all the loves and father's care is the father of all the cares.**

She not only bears your weight but also shares her blood and flesh with you. You get a heart; you get a head; you get a chest; you get a stomach; you get a pair of hands; you get a pair of legs, and your entire body is formed from her blood and flesh. You grow slurping her blood. You grow gulping her power. You suck her energy and squeeze her strength for your survival and growth! You develop yourself inside making her poor outside. You are growing inside, but she is becoming feeble and fragile outside. Despite her physical weakness, she holds you tight and supports you all day and night. She doesn't let you go even when you are slurping her blood and sucking all her power. Isn't it simply invaluable? How do you calculate the cost of this effort? How do you fix the value of her struggle? What level of respect does she deserve for her tolerance, patience, pain, and time? And how do you value the man who stands like a strong pillar and shoulders all her pain and problems during her pregnancy. He manages all her emotions and offers his shoulder to rest on. He takes her to the hospital for regular check-ups and for ultrasound scans. He ensures that there are always enough fruits, vegetables, and nuts at home and tries his best to be around her. He makes her feel special and does everything to make her journey of pregnancy memorable. How do you gauge the value of all this and what do they deserve in return? We certainly think twice before offering a penny to someone, but she literally offers you everything, and he literally does all the things necessary to bring you on earth safely. **She even puts her own life at risk! And he dedicates his whole life for your sake.**

Remember that you were delivered after tolerating intolerance. As soon as they see you in their hands, they get attached to you. They start liking you and love you abundant. They take care of you; they nurse you; they wake up at midnight to check if you are sleeping well; they change your wet clothes; they clean your face, mouth, eyes, ears, nose, hands, legs, and every part of your body. They feed you when you cry; they clean you when you poop; and they take you to the doctor when you are not normal. They feel happy when you laugh; they dance when you dance; they scream when you scream; they blink when you blink; they sleep when you sleep; they wake up when you wake up, and they eat when you eat. **They literally serve you as if they are your paid servants, they work for you as if they are your bondage labourers and they endure all the inconveniences, troubles and disturbances like mother earth for you.** Don't you think they deserve respect? They have not only passed their schools without google and You tube but also graduated without AI apps ?.

But being their beloved child, whom do you like and love abundant? Whom are you attached to? Whom do you always keep with you and care for? Whom do you clean and keep safe? Whom do you often check if everything is okay and comfortable? What do you regularly monitor to see if everything is fine and fit? And whom do you look after with love and care? Do you know the answer? Is it your father? Or is it your mother? No. It's neither your father nor mother, but your mobile phone and its charger! Do you agree? If so, **are we getting more attached to devices than dear ones?** Has importance shifted from people to products? Do we prefer machines over humans? And are we more committed to what we like than to who likes us? By the way, what about you?

Of course, giving birth is a challenging and difficult job, but managing and maintaining a baby after that is even more difficult and challenging. It keeps moving; it keeps doing something; it keeps thinking somewhat and keeps itself busy doing all kinds of unwanted things all the time. It is tough to monitor a child 24 hours a day and difficult to handle it all day. Believe it or not, **it's a difficult and frustrating full-time job for years.** But your parents forget their frustration, pain, and irritation when you just look at them; when you smile at them; when you come near to them; when you cry for them, and when you call them for help or food. They just leave everything, forget what they are doing, and rush towards you.

Do you know how much attention they must have paid for your safety; How much stress they may have taken to take care of your health, body, and mind. How much caution and precaution they must have taken to bring you up properly and how much effort they must have put in to build your future. Value their selfless care and unconditional love. **Don't just be in their house, bein their heart too.**

They do not simply deliver you like an online shopping delivery agent does a product to your door. They work for you until you start working; they earn for you until you start earning; they live for you until you start living;

they walk for you until you start walking; they talk for you until you start talking, and they stand for you until you start standing for yourself. They don't stop doing it even after you are grown up. They continue to talk for you; they continue to walk for you, they continue to earn for you, they continue to stand for you, and they continue to work you in one or the other way.

They take you to school and let you study. They take you to your favourite restaurant and let you to eat. They take you to ice cream parlour and get you the one. They take you out for shopping and let you buy. They take you to playground and let you play. They take you to parks and allow you to have fun. They drive you to the bakery and get you a piece of cake. They take you to the shop and get you chocolates.

They take you to movie theatres and let you watch your favourite one. They take you to the library and allow you to read. They take you on tour and let you enjoy. They take you on a trip and let you relax. They tell you about God and let you pray.

They work so that you can play. They earn so that you can spend. They prepare food so that you can eat. **They work hard so that you can sleep well. They face the sun so that you can be in shadow. They confront the wind so that you can enjoy the breeze. They absorb the heat to keep you cool. They teach the lessons so that you can learn. They let you learn so that you can earn.**

But they scold you sometimes, so that you should not get scolded by others; They teach you so that you should not be taught by others; They act strict so that you can learn discipline. They spend their money for you so that you should not beg others. They help you so that you should not look at others for help. They fulfil all your needs and try to satisfy your wants so that you should not get misused by others. **First, they give you your life and then they give you theirs.**

They not only give what we need but also try to get what we want. **They not only spend their money on us but also spend their time.** They not only love but also sacrifice for our well-being.

If you fight with your friends, you are no longer their friend; if you fight with your colleagues, they may stop talking to you; if you fight with your neighbours, they may start hating you; if you fight with your relatives, they may start troubling you; If you fight with your employer, you may not remain their employee, but **if you fight with your mother, she remains your mother, and if you fight with your father, he remains your father.**

Now, do you have enough reasons to respect your parents? If your answer is "no" or if you think that these reasons are not sufficient to respect them, then you must wait. You must wait until you become a father of your own child; you must wait until you become a mother of your own baby; wait to know the sacrifices they made; wait to understand the risks they took; wait to realise the emotions they went through; wait to realize the loss they incurred; wait to know the quantity of happiness they lost, and wait to understand the quality of love they showered. Wait until your children are born and wait until your children are grown. Wait to experience the difficulties that they give; wait to go through the emotions that they provoke; wait to understand the immense love that you show on them, wait to realise the intense care that you take for them, and wait to realise the depth of your emotional attachment with them.

But please keep this in mind that your parents are not the permanent members of this world and do not stay with us forever. They have already spent nearly 50% of their lives and 50% only is remaining. Time will not wait; it runs fast and doesn't have patience. So, don't wait till you become parent to realize the value of your parents. Understand it early and do what is necessary.

Be grateful to your parents for what they have done and are doing for you. They have given their time, their name, and their energy. They have dedicated their age, health, and wealth. They have lost their happiness, peace for you and have given up many of their desires, wants, and wishes for your sake and for your bright future.

So, they certainly deserve your respect. And it must be given. But do you know how to respect them? It can be demonstrated at its best by adhering to their advices. Respect can be shown just by listening to them silently, by understanding them quietly without interrupting in between. Think before you cut them short and listen to them with the intention of understanding what they are saying. **Listen to understand rather than to respond**. In most cases, children hear their parents to reply or argue. Don't always be in the defensive mood and never always be busy in justifying your actions and attitude. Don't always be quick to justify your actions, and never be in a hurry to defend yourself. Do it only if it is necessary. **Understand first and response is next.** Your attitude, your response, your action, and your reaction may change the moment you understand why they are saying "what they are saying."

Parents should be respected through your behaviour, mind, and speech. You can show your respect in many ways, like how you sit in front of them, how you conduct yourself in their presence, how you speak with them, how you respond to them, and how you react to them. But respect is not just about how you stand or sit in front of them. **Respect is not just about how you treat your parents but also about how others treat them because of you.** Are theygetting applauded because of your good behaviour and character? Are they being appreciated because of your good actions and attitude? Are they getting admired because of your deeds, dedication, and dutifulness? Are they getting praised because of your manners, culture, and rites? and are they being asked **"How to raise our children like your son or daughter?".** Yes. **knowledge may give you power but character brings you respect.**

It is called respect when others around you regard your parents because of the reason that they are your parents. It is called respect when others around you value your parents because of the values that you follow. It is called respect when you make your society respect them through your work. It is called respect when you make people around you respect them because of your culture, values, patience, performance, conduct and achievement. And it is known as respect when your society respects them because of your success, duty, service, help, and patriotism.

It is respect when your parents are recognized for their contributions and perseverance behind your success. It is an honour when one appreciates your parents for your greatness. It is a mark of respect when your father and mother are honoured for your contribution to society, nation and the humanity.

It is an honorary moment for them when they hear about your sincerity, responsibility, and honesty. It is a moment of pride for them when people speak about your help, support, gratitude, and greatness. It's a big moment for them when their relatives and friends respect them for being your parents. But the best way to bring respect to your parents is to make them feel proud and honoured for being your parents. **Nevermake them feel, "Why the hell we give birth to this person?". Never make them think "What was the blunder we did to get this kind of a son or daughter?" and not even once create a situation where they are forced to bow their heads out of shyness and disrespect.**

One of the greatest means of showing respect to them is to ensure that your parents are never ashamed of you, your work, your behaviour, your character, or your existence. Ensure that no one else on earth disrespect, humiliates, dishonours, or insults your parents because of the reason that you are their son or daughter.

There will always be a difference between you and them. There will always be differences between their beliefs and your beliefs. There will always be a conflict between your point of view and their point of view. There will always be a gap between your theories and theirs. There will always be a disparity between the way you think, and they. But be mindful about your actions and reactions while handling such situations. **Remember that your children learn from you and treat you the way you treat your parents.** There will always be dissimilarities and disagreement between you and them and There will always be dispute between what is right and what is wrong. But be mindful about the language that you use and the tone that you raise while expressing your disagreement. **Remember that your children will learn from you and behave the way you behave with your parents.** If you don't respect your parents, how others will respect them? and if you don't treat them well, how others will do? So, your first gift is to treat them with respect all the time.

.

Save the Head

.

Respect those hands
worked for you
Respect those legs
walked for you

.

Respect those eyes
cried for you
Respect the heart
beat for you

.

Respect those fingers
wiped your tears
Respect those shoulders
Carried your fears

.

Respect to her
She gave birth to you
Respect to him
He gave life to you

.

Respect to them
For the love shown
Respect to them
For the care given

.

Serve the life, served you
Save the head, saved you

Respect the sacrifices made for you
And respect the life lived for you

.

CHAPTER TWO

LOVE

"Love" is nothing but an intense feeling of deep affection towards someone or something. The only love that is truly unconditional and selfless is parental love. No love is greater than mother's love and no care is bigger than father's care. They love us wholeheartedly, no matter how much pain we may have caused them. They love us unconditionally, no matter how much trouble we may have given them, and they love us selflessly, no matter how selfish we are.

Love starts between you and your mother when she becomes pregnant. This love connection turns out to be unbreakable when you continue to grow in her womb. The intensity of love increases when she starts breast feeding you and the ever-lasting relationship get stronger and stronger when you start pouncing mother to call her. But for a father, it's love at first sight. The love connection becomes unbreakable when he holds the dew fresh new-born baby in his hands for the first time and hugs you to his heart. The intensity of love rises when you start responding to him on his gestures, voice, and actions. And the everlasting bonding get stronger and stronger when you start pronouncing father to call him.

Soon after your birth, you start depending on them. And this dependency gradually gets converted into love. So, you no need to put in extra effort to love your parents, it comes naturally. They will become your first love inevitably. You start liking them without your own knowledge, you start loving them without even knowing what love is and what it means. But it doesn't come out of dependency in their case because it's a pure love. **Their love is well thought, matured, full-fledged and committed**.

You will come to know about your parents before you know yourself. You will start understanding your parents before you understand yourself and you start loving your parents before you love yourself. Because they are there as soon as you cry, they are there as soon as you lough, they are there as soon as you scream, they are there as soon as you sneeze, they are there as soon as you cough, they are there as soon as you need something, they are there before you close your eyes in the night and they are there before you open your eyes in the morning. They are the first ones you see as soon as you wake up, the first voice you hear is theirs; the first touch you feel is theirs; and theirs is the first love that you experience. It's like one soul in three bodies. In fact, you become them, and they become you. **The state of true love.**

You are loved every day; You are helped at every step, and you are shown the unconditional affection throughout your life. **Nobody on earth can ever love you more than your parents. No one can ever care you better than them and no one on earth can tolerate you more than them.**

Your first cry, your first smile, when they look into your eyes for the first time and when you bite their finger from your teethless month for the first ever are special experience to them. When she hears you calling mom for the first time, when dad is heard for the first occasion and when you rush to hug them as soon as they get home are their beautiful moments. Your first stage performance, your first competition, the first prize you won and the first gift you gave are their sweet memories. The first love that you show, the first hug that you gave, the first job you got. the first salary you brought, the first car you bought, the first house you built are their happiest events of life. Your first marriage and the first child of yours bring them unbearable happiness and are unforgettable memories that they cherish for life.

Children are always lucky in this parent-child relationship, they are on the safer side of the relationship and are big beneficiaries of this relationship by default. They are deeply loved and well cared by their parents all the time without expectation. No matter how old you get, they love you and support you. Along with their love and support, they also give you their name, their time, their knowledge, their wealth, their property, and their legacy at free of cost. And all this contribution comes in the name of love. But **the responsibility of keeping their love alive lies with you. So, reciprocate positively and cherish that rare love.**

Do you know that they get scared when you come home late? Do you know they feel uncomfortable when you are not in comfort? Do you know that they get nervous when you are not normal? You know they feel sad when you are not happy? You know they feel the pain while you are suffering? You know they get restless when you are not at peace? You know they get strained when you are disappointed, and they get disappointed when you are depressed. They get anxious when you are sick, and they feel sick when you are out of sync? They feel injured when you are hurt, and they get angry when someone ill-treat. Do you know why? And what is the reason behind such doings? It's their selfless love and immense affection.

Your mother feels as if she herself is hungry when you tell her that you are hungry. No matter what condition she is in, no matter what important work she is doing, no matter how much her head is aching at that point in time, she gets up like a soldier and goes straight to the kitchen, looking for utensils to prepare food for you. She prepares quickly and serves in no time. Waits for you to finish so that she can serve again. This happens in the name of love. And this happens every day in every home. Your father feels the pain when you say you are hurt. He rushes for your help, aid and extend his helping hand.

They not only love you immensely but also pray for you. Probably, they are the only people on earth who prays for you and for your well-being. **Can you think of anyone else?** [Stop reading and think for a minute on this. Write down the name if you get any]

But as you grow up and start experiencing new aspects of life, your parents may gradually become a part of your life, but you remain their life.They may slowly become part of your world, but you remain their world.But it doesn't mean that they don't have their own life and their own world other than you. They have their own lives; they have their own world but what it means is that **you are your parents' top priority as long as you need them. But in other's cases, you become their top priority only when they feel they need you.**

Sometimes, without understanding the above truth, we give too much of importance to others. Though we love our parents immensely, we ignore their love and snub their affection many times because of other people and other things.

We love them dearly as long as we are small; we love them immensely until our mind is matured; we love them unconditionally until we gain the power of thinking of our own; we love them infinitely as long as we are not exposed to outside world; we love them enormously as long as we have no external attractions, and we love them extremely as long as we are dependent on them. But the actual change starts when you start thinking on your own! The importance of your parents begins to diminish as you grow older, and experience new attractions of life. Their prominence begins to reduce as we mature. And we start finding problems in their love and start looking for flaws in their affection. **Their significance fades when you begin to realize that they are no longer inevitable, and their value diminishes when you begin to feel that they are not necessary anymore for your survival. Is it true in your case as well!?**

Especially during your teenage, you need to ensure that your roots are still in ground. You need to remind yourself that the importance and significance should continue to be given to your parents too. Though your love gets scattered as you grow, their love gets intensified. Though your priorities change in your teenage, you remain their priority. Though you yearn for new relationships and bad habits, they try to restrain and regulate your crazy mind. When they try to regulate your mind and thought, you may get irritated and annoyed. But, be mindful about what you speak and how you behave with them during that time. **Don't get into arguments all the time, it affects the love and never let your egos spoil the relation, it may detach the attachment.** Ensure that theroots of your relationship stand firm while you are sailing in the crazy stream of teenage youth.**Many times, we get into trouble not because of what we say but how we say. Be mindful of your body language and tone when you are hot headed.**

The new weather, new people, new exposure, new opportunities, new habits, new hobbies, new wants, new desires, new friends, new feelings, new freedom, and new interests not only start **taking priority in your teenage life but also starts driving you crazy.** All these new attractions come with extreme force. It rushes like a rocket and pushes you like an elephant. It becomes too difficult for you to control it and its speed. At the same time, it becomes too challenging for them to fulfil all your insane wants and emotional desires. The aggression and the craziness of new attractions of your teenage life would blindfold you and suffocate them. So, curb your crazy desires, wishes, and lust. Command your body and control your mind. Never let it jump like a monkey in the stream of infatuation. Tame it, govern it, and drive it in the right direction.

Your 'new attractions and insane desires' on side and their 'responsibilities' on the other side, both together may put pressure on parent-child relationship, and it starts adversely affecting the rapport between you and them. Since theirresponsibility comes with lot of responsibility and your new attractions are intensely attractive, relationship may struggle to survive. During this sensitive phase, put in extra effort to keep your desires and expectations in control and try hard to hold the relationship solid and strong.

Though their love is the only love that is truly unconditional, selfless, and forgiving, the relationship suffers when their responsibility collides with your irresponsibility. When responsibility starts riding on their shoulder, their talk, walk and behaviour change. When you make mistakes, they try to correct. When you make faults, they try to rectify. When you make errors, they try to fix and when you make blunder, they try to repair. But it may not go down well with you. You may get irritated by their correction and may easily get frustrated by their rectification. You may get annoyed when they try to fix your behavioural issues and may easily get vexed when they try to repair your attitude. Yes. Your young and immature mind may not accept their intervention and their intrusion in your matter. Instead, your mind wants them to hug you, kiss you, and show you the love even when you are repeating your mistakes, making faults, and committing blunders one after the other. **But it is necessary for them to hold the stick of teaching in one hand and the flower of love in the other.** Although it's tough to use both beating stick and the flower of love at the same time, but inevitable for them.

Besides fulfilling your needs, wants, and wishes, they also have to manage their own personal desires, problems, work pressure, financial matters, social disputes, and family issues on the other side. Usually, children would neither have the burden of 'responsibility' nor the 'pressure' of life. They will always be in fun and party mood. But the case is different with parents. **They have to bear not only the burden of responsibility but also to face the intensity of stress.** When they try to teach you lessons, they look like villains, but when they ignore your mistakes, they look irresponsible. Isn't it hard to balance?

As and how you grow, the weight of your responsibility increases on them. When it completely falls on their shoulder, they get busy schooling you, preparing food for you, teaching you manners, providing education, training social etiquettes, choosing right path, taking right decision, fulfilling your needs, satisfying your wants, meeting your expectations, matching your wavelength, behaving according to your mood, controlling your anger, managing your frustration, handling your stupidity, dealing with your innocence, coping up with your emotions, tolerating your nonsense, accepting your mistakes, digesting your failures, bringing you back on track of success, earning money for you, managing your expenses and building assets for your future. etc. etc. Don't feel left out and don't let the roots of relationship go loose when they get busy in their duties and get occupied in carrying out their responsibilities.

Children think that their parents are broad-minded as long as no questions are raised on their behaviour and freedom. They feel that their parents are good as long as they accept their demands and fulfil all their wishes. Parents are smooth hearted as long as they don't ask anything about their mistakes, faults, and flaws. And parents are great as long as they don't talk about their duties, manners, and responsibilities. But the same relationship may start to deteriorate when a father begins to teach them responsibility and mother begins to teach them the culture and sacrament.

Yes. When a father begins to teach responsibilities, the strong roots of the relationship may begin to shake. Yes. When a mother starts educating their children on their culture, customs and sacrament, the roots of a relationship shake. Children just want them to be left free. They think that these culture and customs are outdated; sacraments are based on blind beliefs. It is not prevalent for them and is of no use in the modern society. They are not in the mood to understand their responsibility and accountability; rather, they will be in their own world of enjoyment, fun, and entertainment. They always want to be free. They expect their parents to keep giving them what they want and keep doing what they tell. They just don't want to work hard; they don't want to get disturbed when they are flying high in their own fantasy world and they don't want to be bothered by anyone when they are in their comfort and at ease.

But they don't know that, such attitude will have a negative impact on their growth. Such viewpoint may wreck their present, and such arrogance may spoil their future. The resistance to practise our culture and protest to take up the responsibility will bring cracks in relationships, and related arguments may lead to disputes. So, don't make the same mistake when your parents try to teach you what is important for your life. **Follow your culture and be ready to shoulder the burden of your own responsibility.**

It is told that God created parents because he cannot be everywhere to love and care. But parents too can't stay with us forever. And they too leave us in between. But they don't want us to leave us alone. They don't like us to be lonely and alone after their death. Questions like, "What next? Who will continue to love you after their death? And who will care and look after you till your death?" trouble them and bother them. Since they know that they cannot live, love and care for us until our end, they start searching for someone who can love us till the end. They start looking for a someone who can take care of us throughout the life and stand firm with us till the end of our life. They try their best to find the best suitable one for you and go beyond their limits to pick the right one for you. They look for someone who can be the best companion throughout your life and can take good care of you even after the end of their life.

But looks like some young ones are in hurry. They don't wait for the right time and right age. They yearn for new relationships at the early stage of their life and suffer badly later. They don't understand that such attractions may spoil their education, goal, future and will wreck their personal life too.

Unfortunately, few adult children go to next level. They cheat their own parents by getting married without even informing their parents. They act as if nothing has happened in their life and stay quiet about it. They behave as if they don't know anything about what they have done. But the innocent parents continue to believe them and their drama. This is the height of betrayal and massacre of parents' love and trust. Such behaviour depresses and humiliates and keep insulting them lifelong. **However, this does not preclude you from selecting your life partner or falling in love with someone of your choice. But wait until the right time and do it in the right way.** You can very well choose your life partner and you have all the rights to do so but wait for the right age and do it in the right way with the right sense of awareness and responsibility. Don't betray your parents and never play with their emotions, instead take them into your confidence while taking any such major decisions of life.

The reason we studied is our parents; the reason we survived is our parents; the reason we are alive today is our parents; The hands that supported us were those of our parents; the shoulders that lifted us belonged to our parents; the pair of legs that walked for us were of our parents; and the voice that instilled confidence and courage in us was the voice of our parents. The body worn out in our service is the body of our parents, and the mind that got exhausted thinking about us is our parents' mind. And the eyes that cried for us were related to our parents. **But when it's your turn to return their love, affection, and care, will**

you back down or stand firm with them?

Before you think about returning their love and care, do you know what your parents expect from you in return of their unconditional love, care, and affection?

Wow. That's an interesting question! Because they should not expect anything in return, if their love and care is unconditional. Right?

Yes. Good point! But it does not mean that you should not give back anything in return. **Irrespective of whether they expect it from you or not, regardless of what they like to get it from you or not, they deserve a return gift.** Do you agree?If so, what is it? Instead of thinking from their perspective on what they want in return, think from your perspective what you owe them.

Irrespective of what they expect or whether they accept or not, it's your duty to return the same amount of love and care. Try your best to give your best and return their love and care with respect. **How can you expect from your children what you can't give your parents?**

Your tireless and all-day working mom may depend on you one day; your world's strongest man may struggle to take a step forward another day. He may drop food while eating, she may spill water while drinking, and they may ask the same question three times and one more time. They may tell you two times whatever they have already told you three times. They may need your support to go to the bathroom and may need your presence around them to survive. Though your heart aches to see them in such condition, you may get irritated, you may get annoyed, and you may even feel disgusting. But the ask is to patiently understand their condition and do the necessary. **If you can't change the situation, change yourself.** Be patient, cool, calm, and compassionate. It may not be so easy, but necessary. Understand the need of the hour and do what it takes. **Remember that the beginning of every new phase is always a challenge.**

After a stage, their childhood returns, and they may behave childish. So, love your parents like how you love your children; treat your parents as you would treat your own offspring. Show the commitment that you show towards your spouse and take care of your parents as you would your children and house. Never hate them, never trouble them, and never leave them when they need your presence around them. They have certainly forgotten and forgiven many of your mistakes, faults, and sins. Forgive them for theirs if any. **Its okey if you can't love them but never hate them.** Its okey if you don't make them feel loved and proud but never make them feel, "Why the hell did we give birth to this person?" or "What was the sin we did to get such a son?" or "What crime did we commit to get a daughter like one". **If you are a good son, remain their son even after your marriage and children. If you are a good daughter, remain their daughter even after your teenage, marriage and daughter.**

Ensure that they are loved when they are alive, and make sure that your love is visible before they go invisible. Be expressive; don't hesitate to express your love for your parents. Usually, adult children hesitate to express their love openly and keep it to themselves. But it is good to show your love. Give hugs, give gifts, give kisses, and put your arms around them. Say, "I love you so much", "You are simply great", "Thank you very much", and "It means a lot to me" as and when you feel so. Treat them how you like to be treated by your children and love them how you like to be loved by your children. Treat them how they treated you when you were their children and love them how they loved you when you were their smaller one.Show your gratitude and be grateful for what they have done and for what they have given you.

You can consider yourself debt free only when you return what you receive. If you don't want to return, don't take it. But if you have already taken, don't betray but return. [Pause reading. Close your eyes and think about what you have received from whom and when will you return it.] **Return what you receive and return more if you can.** Remember that you have not only received from your father, mother, siblings, friends, and colleagues but also from your nation, nature, and mother earth. So, what are you planning to give back to all of them?

.

What Shall I Do Now?

.

I feel like stopping my mom form regular
And prepare breakfast for her
I feel like holding my dad's hand
And take him out for dinner

.

I feel like crying before my mom
And tell her all my pain
I feel like hugging my dad
And share all my problem

.

I feel like taking a long leave
Just to be with my mom
I feel like relaxing my head
on my father's bosom

.

I feel like building them a new house
And be with them for ever
I feel like buying them a new car
And go on tour for ever

.

But They can't hear me now
And I can't see them now
Neither they can come down
Nor I can go up

.

Do what you would like to do
When they are with you
Do what you would wish to do
When they are around you

.

They don't stay with us till the end
Once gone, God will not resend
They don't stay with us till the end
Once gone, will not resend

.

CHAPTER THREE

LISTEN

Parents have learnt a lot from their experiences; they have understood a lot dealing with different people; they have realized a lot going through different situations; they have grasped a lot from different circumstances; they have perceived a lot from different challenges, and they can look at the things differently from different perspectives. Yes. The time and experience have made them good teachers. Learning has made them better than us and knowledge has made them wiser than us. Therefore, they can play the role of a better teacher for your bright future. **That is why it is said that home is the first school and parents are the first teachers.**

They teach us to raise early; they teach us to work hard; they teach us to study well; they teach us to behave well; they teach us to be strong; they teach us to be brave; they teach us to be honest, and they teach us the importance of family, they tach us to respect our culture, and they teach us to respect and care elderly. Yes. They teach us a lot from the beginning of our life till the end of their life.

They teach us how to be grateful; they teach us how to be respectful, and they teach us how to be thankful. They teach us why to be punctual; they teach us why to be honest and they teach us how to be humble. They teach us how to admit our mistakes and what to be learnt from it. They teach us why to take care of our health and how to be happy. They teach us why to select good friends and be one. They teach us how to aim high and achieve it. They teach us to be generous but stay in control. They teach us to take responsibilities but not to overcommit. They tell us not to run behind money but work hard to earn more. And they teach us to spend money but wisely. Yes. They teach us almost everything we need to live our life on our own strength. They teach us money management; they teach us time management and they also cover emotion management. They teach us almost all that we need to lead a respectful and successful life. So, promise that "I listen to my parents and follow their teachings".

Their brain is fully developed; their thoughts are wholly matured; they may already be fully aware of the consequences of an action that you are planning to take, and they may already know the results of your decisions that you are going to make. So, listen to them. **Their guidance can change your life and their directions can make your life.**

Luckily, whether we want it or not, whether we are interested or not, they advise us and guide us. Whether we like it or not, they keep telling us and educating us. But unfortunately, children do not listen to them all the time and ignore them most of the time. Since it is a free advice, we do not take it seriously. But their guidance and advice can make us right, straight, and great; their warning can stop us from making mistakes; their caution can save us from failures, their suggestion can help us reach our goals, their alerts can avoid major problems and can lead to the pinnacle of success. Hence, pay attention to what they say. **Since they know you better, they can guide you better.**

But most of the time, children do not even hear what is being said. They do not have the patience to sit, listen, and understand what is being told. True that It's a busy world. Everyone is busy. Some are busy with work, and some without. Most of the time, we found ourselves busy talking to someone on mobile, texting somebody, watching something on TV, browsing our mobile all the time, working on our laptop, or thinking about something or someone while our parents are speaking to us. We will always be busy in doing one or the other things. If so, does it mean that we do not have enough time to pay attention to our parents? Or does it mean that we are busy giving importance to everything else other than our own parents? **Listening is one of the genuine ways of showing respect.** The quieter you become, the more you can listen. The more you listen, quieter you become. Yes. when you know more, you will be calmer and when you know more, you will listen more.

Most of the time, **we take them for granted**. don't we!? Somehow, we have taken that freedom, or they may have given us that liberty. But it is not right and is one of the biggest mistakes that most of us easily make. We expect them to do all the things for us, but we find all the reasons to blame them. We think that everything is their duty, and all that they are doing for us is their responsibility. But we fail to understand that **we are not here only to fly high like free birds all the time but also to take responsibility of our own life.**

But the basic question here is why should I listen to my parents? Why? why should I? Why can't I live the way I want1? Why can't I do what I would like to do? Why can't I behave the way I like to? Why can't I react the way I feel like? Is it just because they are my parents? Or is it just because they are taller than me? Or is it because they are elder than me or because they are old? Or is it just to make them feel good? No, it's not just because they're your biological parents; it's not just because they're elders; it's not just to make them happy; but **they know more than that of you know and they understand what's best for you. Their advice is to help you and to make your life easier and better. Listen to your parents irrespective of whether you agree with them or not. They may not always be right but might have learnt from doing wrong.**

Actively listening makes them or any speaker feel valued and happy. It not only builds trust and makes relationships stronger but also reduces misunderstandings. It shows how much we care and respect them.

Means, should I listen to them just to show some respect and care? No. It's not just to show them respect or care, but also to learn and understand our life better. They know us more than we know ourselves. They have our best interests at heart. They only want to keep us away from troubles and struggles and they simply want us to have a better life. So, listening to them can avoid problems, can give us confidence, and can make our life easier. It can turn our worries into happiness and can transform our problems into opportunities. True that it irritates when our parents keep telling us same thing over and over again, but don't neglect. It's ok to pretend rather ignoring them while they are speaking to you. **If you understand whatever is being said is being said for our good, then there will not be any doubt whether I should listen to them or not.**

We may know more than them in few subjects and we may be better in few topics due to our higher education, advancements in technology and communications, but our parents have more experience in life than we do. They may have already gone through what we are going through now. They may have already seen what we are experiencing now. Though, they may not be able to solve your entire problem but can certainly point you in the right direction or can give hints of solution. **Though we are advanced in science and technology today, we still have to go through the same emotions and similar situations that they have already gone through. Human feelings and emotions remain the same from generation to generation; only the environment, situations, people, and reasons change.**

They may or may not be graduates or hold any high position in society, but they have more experience in life; they have more knowledge about people; they know more about society. They have met and seen more people than you. Their experience with people has made them wiser than you, and their interaction with individuals has made them cleverer. Moreover, they know what is best for us. They can analyse the situation better and make the best decision for us. Because they know our strengths, they know our weaknesses, and are fully aware of our capabilities. Hence, they can guide us better than anyone else. Sometimes we think that our parents don't understand what we are going through, but they do, and they can. Because they have already gone through it. They are the ones who assured us and filled us with confidence that everything would be all right, no matter what happened. **Sometimes, their advice sounds like watching commercials on TV. You know what is coming but listen anyway.**

They have already seen the same life that you have just started to see now. They may have a better understanding of what is right and what is wrong. They may already know the consequences of your actions and reactions. They may have made errors and understood how to correct it. They may have committed same mistakes and learned lessons; they might have faced difficult situations and overcome from them. They may have successfully handled the same troubles earlier and may have already met the same challenges before. So, they may know how to handle the situation better than you. Hence, acknowledge and accept the fact that they are better than you. Yes, they are better than us in many matters. May not be in all matters, but for sure, they are better than us in many matters of life. **Listening is an art that requires trust than ego. It's an art of understanding what is being said and why it is being said. So, listen with attention rather than ego.**

Remember that your parents were also children; they were adolescents; they were teens too and only after that they became adults! They have gone through that age, they have gone through that experience, they have gone through the similar feelings, and they have gone through the same emotions and pressure. They know what it's like to be in your shoes.

They can see your life from an outsider's perspective to make a suitable suggestion. They have the ability to see the whole picture and they will never let you go in the wrong direction. So, listen to what they have got to say. They genuinely care about you. **Remember that every rule they establish, every restriction they put, and every hurdle they create are just to keep you safe, clean, and happy.** It's always better to listen than to regret later.

Listen to them because you can completely believe them and can trust them more than anyone. Your parents may or may not know about computers, latest apps, or new technologies, but they have more experience in life. They know how tough life is getting day by day, and they may have clues on how to handle it better and how to be prepared for new challenges and risks in life.

Our parents simply want us to have a good life. **Our success and our well-being are the only intentions that they have.** They care our life and can repair if necessary.

Above all, what do they tell us to listen? Do they ask us to take wrong route? Do they tell us to go against what is good? Do they pressure us to follow something immoral or illegal? Or do they motivate us to do something which can ruin our future? After all, what do they expect us to listen and follow? Why are we so apathetic about it? Do they tell us to be harmful and hate yourself? **No! Not at all.** Theyalways advise us to eat well, be healthy, study hard, do good, be good, work well, be honest, and behave properly. If all their advice sounds good and make sense! Then, what is the problem in following it?

We have seen people lose their jobs, respect and status because of their bad manners and lack of etiquette. We have observed people lose their positions because of their absurd behaviours, and we have seen people lose their business because of their conduct and character. Today, if you are leading a respectful life without any such stains, it means that **it is because of the rite that they gave you.** It's because of the culture that they taught you, and it's because the strong foundation that they laid for you. Yes. The first thing they teach us is manners and etiquette.

They ask us to get up early in the morning. They tell us to do exercise and get involved in physical activities for our health. When you start suffering from back pain or any other health issues later, you realize the value of their advice. When a person gets up early, he gets more time, fresh air, a calm mind, a peaceful environment, and there are many more advantages. Research conducted by Texas

University has identified that students who were early risers scored better grades than those who were late to rise. **And another piece of research has also suggested that people who get up early are happier throughout the day.**

They caution you to keep yourself away from junk foods. Frequently eating more junk food is linked to a higher risk of obesity, depression, digestive issues, heart disease, stroke, diabetes, cancer, and even early death.

They always advise us not to smoke and not to drink alcohol. Smoking can damage your organs; it may lead to kidney and throat cancer. It can damage our lungs. It also raises our blood pressure and cholesterol levels, it reduces bone density, and increases the risk of infertility. It may cause preterm delivery, stillbirth, and sudden infant death. Heavy alcohol consumption can lead to many serious health conditions. Binge drinking can cause immediate problems like nausea, vomiting, blurred vision, and impaired judgment. In the long term, heavy alcohol consumption can cause high blood pressure, gastric problems, liver cirrhosis, liver cancer, memory impairment, alcohol dependence, and various psychological conditions. Excessive alcohol consumption can also result in accidental injuries and death.

They tell us not to watch TV too much. Too much screen time can lead to obesity, sleep problems, chronic neck, and back problems in children. You will understand the value of their advice when you meet doctors due to these concerns.

They complain about cell phone usage and advise us not to use them excessively. You may suffer from headache, eye strain, shortness of temper, sleep disorder, neck problem, depression, anxiety loss of sense of time, chronic stress, sleep loss, Cyberbullying, obesity, and vison problems.It not only harms your personal physical and mental health but also harms your family and culture. **Excessive use of mobile phones not only puts your health at risk but also destroys your relationships like slow poison.**

They tell us to select good friends. Bad friends may hurt you badly, you may get trapped in unwanted matters and may get dragged into unnecessary issues. You may even get jailed in bad friendship. Sometimes, it may even take your life too. So, it's better to be alone than in bad company. So, they tell you to choose friends carefully and always associate yourself with good friends and people.

They warn us to be cautious about new relationships, infatuation, love, affairs, and so on. New relationships during studies or at young age destroy your concentration, focus, and goals. It diverts you from your aim and purpose. Moreover, those who get involved in new relationships at a young age cannot deal with it. It's so dangerous that even adults have failed to deal with it! A toxic relationship may negatively impact your physical and mental health. And negative relationships put people at a higher risk of developing heart problems. Researchers found that people with high levels of conflict in their relationships tend to have high blood sugar levels, high blood pressure, and high rates of obesity. There may be other physical repercussions too, in the form of stress, constant tension, and organ damages etc.,

They want you to be happy. They advise us to be independent and not to depend on anyone. **The guilt of being burden on someone harasses us all the time throughout life. The dependency on others always lead to disappointment and it enslaves. Even your own open eyes can't help you in your darkness.**

They encourage to be successful. They ask you to help people. They tell you to do good for your society and they may tell you to work for mankind. They teach you to be patriot and love your nation.

They warn you to stay away from bad things, bad habits, bad people, and bad activities. **But, without understanding the care and purpose behind their guidance, we begin to dislike them! Instead, listen to them for your own benefit.** It helps you. It supports you; it gives you power, strength, confidence, and courage. Moreover, it safeguards you and secures your future. **Listen to them not just because they are always right but because they have learnt from being wrong.**

"Listen to understand, not to reply." It's hard to understand when you are thinking about giving a solid response while someone is talking to you. **If you have observed, the word 'LISTEN' contains the same letters as the word 'SILENT'.** It means that you need to be silent while listening. Because it is hard to listen when you are thinking of a response already.

When you listen to reply rather than understand, then your mind works differently. It starts thinking about how to justify, how to vindicate, and how to prove that you were not wrong. You will get busy choosing right words to respond effectively. You will lose your patience. You will lose your ability to wait till they finish. And you will focus on how to win the war of words against them. So, have patience. Let them finish what they have got to say and wait for them to complete their sentence. If you listen to understand, then you find value in what they are saying. Otherwise, you feel that they are just blaming you and they are trying to prove that you are a culprit. **So, listen, understand, think, and then respond.** Because Listening **is not only about understanding what is being said but more about why it is being said.**

But the important question here is... How long should I listen? **Should I always listen to my parents?** Can't I make my own decision? Don't I have freedom? What about my likes and dislikes? What to do with my desires and aspirations? What to do with my own wants and wishes? I am grown up and I have my own intentions, preferences, goals, and ambitions. Right?

Yes. You have your own intentions, goals, and preferences in life. You do not have to listen to your parents always or forever. They too don't like to see you as their permanent dependent or their follower. They don't expect you to listen to them throughout your life without using your own brain. And they don't expect you to depend on them without doing your own calculations to take your own decisions. **In fact, all that they want in their lives is to see that their children are self-supporting, self-depending, self-relaying, self-determining, self-governing, and happy autonomous power centres.** But always ask their opinion, seek their advice, think through their suggestions, use their counselling, and discuss with them before making your own decision. **It may help you to make a better decision.**

If you don't like their advice or if it is conflicting with your interest or if you have a better idea, then discuss, brainstorm, enquire, ask, questions, ask about their concerns, understand their point of view, and think through being in their shoes. Explain your point of view and reasons behind your decision. Answer any questions they may have. Provide any clarifications they may need. Illustrate the benefits and advantages of your decision if it is being taken against their wishes. Convince and seek their approval before making it final. Compare and prove that your stand is better. If you cannot get their consent and approvals even after that, then follow your conscience. It is not always necessary to act in accordance with their wishes and suggestions. You can carry on with your own decision if you are 100% sure that you are on the right path, you are moving in the right direction, and you are confident about your success.

You can take your own decisions, if you have a better understanding of life, if you have the better judging capability and the capacity to handle the outcome of your choice. You can take your own decisions if you are confident that your decision is better than theirs. You can take your own decisions if you are grown up enough, earned decision-making capabilities, and matured enough to take your own decisions. The important part of decision-making is awareness of its results and the ability to face the consequences of your decisions. When you have a complete understanding of the consequence, effect, and impact of your decision and know how to control and manage it better, then you can make your own decisions.

If you think you have comprehensively matured enough to take your own decisions on your behalf and have all the awareness and knowledge about the consequences, then you can make your own choice without depending on others.

You are free to make your own decisions, but make your parents feel that they hold an important role in your decisions. Make your parents feel that they have a significant place in your heart. **Remember that your parents are the least selfish people around you. And don't forget that It's okey to pretend to listen rather than ignore.**

By the way, how do you respond to your parents when they say something which you don't like? How do you reply to their advice, which you think is outdated and how do you react to their suggestions, which don't make sense to you? How do you act when they go against your ask? How do you react when your request is rejected? How do you reply when tough questions are asked? And how do you behave when they put conditions and ask you to follow rules at home? Do you have enough patience to hold your tongue until they finish their speech? Do you have enough common sense to understand why they act against your wish? Do you have enough awareness to understand why they say "NO"? Or do you get into heated arguments all the time to prove that you are right, and they are wrong. Do you always try to prove that you know better than them? So, what matters is how you react when your parents don't act or react as per your expectations. **Listening is an art that requires more patience than perseverance. And that patience comes only when you quietly understand what is being said and why it is being said.**

.

Listen

.

Listen to your mommy.
She carried you for 9 months.
Listen to your daddy
He carried you for 20 years

.

Listen to your mamma
who gave you the birth
Listen to your dada
who taught how to live until death

.

Listen to your ma

She gave you the love
Listen to your pa
He gave you the life

.

Listen to your mom
She may tell you something sweet
Listen to your dad
He may tell you something great

.

Listen to your mother
She may utter something useful
Listen to your father
He may utter something to be successful

.

Listen to your Amma
She is the best
Listen to your Appa
you can blindly trust

.

CHAPTER FOUR

DEPENDENCY

The next gift is to promise that 'I WILL NOT DEPEND' on my parents after certain period of time. Its fine up to the age 15 but not good after that. Don't expect your parents to clean your room; wash your soiled plates; rinse your dirty clothes and put all your scattered things together even after 15. Instead, do it yourself. Pull your own weight; learn to stand on your own legs, and start helping yourself. **One should depend on oneself, not on others.** The moment you see your parents doing your personal work, you should politely stop them and take it up on your shoulder. Your personal work should only be owned by yourself.

Dependency is injurious to your self-esteem. So, **reduce your dependence on others and take your responsibility yourself.** Adopt **"My work is my duty, and my life is my responsibility"** policy.

In fact, **one should never depend on others, no matter whether the other person is your parents or someone else.** Especially **in financial matters, dependency is strictly forbidden after a point.** Of course, we have been dependent on our parents since our date of birth. So, sudden leap out of it is impossible. But should find ways to come out of it slowly. It is true that reducing financial reliance on parents is difficult, and is a highly challenging task. **But you should slowly start the process of financial independence when you are around 18.** Such attitude leads you towards financial freedom and gives confidence to take decisions on your own behalf. It gives you power. It helps to instil dedication, teaches commitment, encourages self-control, and brings self-discipline in you.

Never become a burden on anyone. Don't let the world look you down. Be dignified, maintain your dignity. Be self-respected, live with self-respect and lead a life of self-esteem always. We have our own hands, legs, brain, and body to help ourselves; we have our own thoughts, mind, and strength to take care of ourselves. And we have our own intellect and power to fulfil our needs and wants. So why to depend on others? Use yourself, your own body and mind to help yourself. Avoid depending on others It showcases your inability and demonstrates your irresponsibility.

If so, how long can I depend on my parents!? You should start taking care of your work when you are around 10. But in case of financial matters, it can go up to 25. By the way, do you know why 25? On what basis the age range of 25–26 is considered as cut-off point in this case? It's purely based on simple mathematics. If you are into studies, it usually takes 22 to 23 years to complete your graduation. Let's add two – three years for your post-graduation or master's degree. On top of it, you may need an extra year to look for a suitable job and settle down. Considering the worst case, one should be able to earn on his own by 26. The best case is soon after 18 –20.

But most of you would be in your schools and colleges at the end of your teenage years 18 - 20. So, how is it possible to earn around 18? Of course, it is difficult. True that it is challenging and may not be an easy task but possible. So,

find ways, not excuses. And if you are not into studies, then you must start your earning by 18.

But, if my parents want me to devote my full time to studies, how can I start my earing around 18?

You are fortunate! It means that your parents are ready to take care of your expenses even after 18. If so, take your education seriously and concentrate on your studies! Don't get diverted; don't get deviated but stay focused and stay committed.

If you continue to depend on them even after 18, then don't spend their money recklessly. Stop the extravagance but start savings. Stop splurging and start helping. **Demand less and save more.** Remember that every penny saved is every penny earned. **So, savings is the best thing that one can do when not in a position to earn.**

By the way, how old are you now? Are your financially independent or dependent on someone? Have you already taken your own responsibility? If not yet, how is the preparation? [Wait, stop reading. Please close the book, close your eyes, think about this question with peace of mind, and put a plan in place.]

Unfortunately, most of the children think that their parents are their private ATMs. They just put their demand in front of them and expect that it should get fulfilled. Even bank ATMs will not honour your demand if there is no sufficient balance in your account. But you would like parents to honour all your requests and demands on time or in no time. Of course, you would like to enjoy your life, you would love to have all the fun on earth, and you would wish to experience all the entertainment around you. **But be sensitive about their limitations and have control on your boundaries.** The environment in which you grow up might give you the confidence that your parents are always there for you to fulfil your wants and wishes. The child-centric family structure might have given you the confidence that parents exist only for the welfare of their children. It's true that your parents are always there for you, but don't misuse their availability. They can only take care of you up to some extent and up to a certain point, but not for ever. **Understand their limitations and business accordingly. never pressurize them.**

Undoubtedly, your life is your right, and you can lead it the way you want, but not at the sweat of your parents' earnings. **Don't forget that your life is not only your right but also your responsibility.**

Don't expect financial help even after 27. Its impotence; its weakness, and powerlessness. Don't look for it and never ask for it. **Don't let your childhood continue even in your adulthood.** Never expect them to take care of you and your expenses even in your adulthood. You would only be the victim of any such expectations. Most of the time, our expectations not only disappoint us but also hurt us badly. It causes unhappiness and unrest within us. Instead, be self-reliant, be self-made and expect more from yourself rather others. **Earn your own money for your spending. Don't expect others to sponsor it. Never forget that the dependence is dangerous, and expectation is fatal.**

Be cautious about your demands and be thoughtful about your expectations. They have grown you up until now and managed all your expenses. **It is not their duty to fund you till your end and manage your expense till their end.Your well-being is your business.** Your inability not only spoil your life but also spoil their left-out life too.

As a grown up, **be careful when you are spending money you never earned.** Financially never remain at the mercy of others. Before expecting or asking for financial help from your parents or someone, keep in mind that they are also responsible for the rest of their life. They need to take care of themselves too, they also have their own wants, wishes, likings, desires, and expenses. In addition to this, they may also be carrying on the responsibilities of their own parents, siblings, spouse, and their other children. So, **never ask anyone for free money. Learn to manage with what you have or earn how much you need. But don't ask anyone. Don't extend your hands in front of others for paper notes. Few may simply deny but few will insult.**

So, never ask money to exhibit your pretentions. Don't look at their sweat money for your show off and never look at their hard-earned money for your ostentatious show. Stay away from such showiness and peacockery. Instead, understand life, focus on your studies, start early preparation, pay attention towards savings, be with the right people, have right attitude, set your goals firmly, make constant progress, and take your life seriously.

Don't always be self-centric. Don't always be focused on your own wants, needs and wishes, but also be mindful about others. They may get ready to help you with their retirement fund; though they may get ready to dissolve their assets at lower valuations for you; though they may get ready to compromise on their comforts and happiness for your wants; though they may unwillingly get ready to get what you want, though they reluctantly get ready to waste their savings on your desires but don't push them to such state and never create such situations.

They have every right to spend each penny of their hard-earned money for their wellbeing. Leading a respectful life in society is their right too. It should never be snatched from them asking for financial help. But some educated or intelligent adult children may politely ask

"Why do you want to waste it? Give it to me; I'll invest it on your behalf!", "Give me your money, I will pay you interest". "Give it to me for high returns". "Give it to me now, I will give it back anytime you want" Etc., [Wait, stop reading. What about you? Have you borrowed money from your parents? Are you seeking financial help from them even in your adulthood?] **Don't lure them for their money but earn your own OR learn to live with what you earn.**

You must have a grip over your spending. **You must have a control over your money; otherwise; it will control you.** If you do not care about money, it doesn't care about you. **Control it before you come under its control and respect it before it disrespects you.** The simple policy that one should adopt in life is "**Live on less than you make.**" This policy not only gives you financial peace but also peace of mind.

While you are dependent on your parents, don't get into new relationships and never get involved in love affairs. It demands money and time. What would you do to keep your new relationships happy? How can you take the responsibility for someone else's happiness without standing on your own legs and without earning your own money? **Don't take on any such responsibilities unless you earn your own money. And never take other's accountability as long as you are reliant on someone else.** Blowing your parents well-earned money on someone or something for your enjoyment is not good. And outlaying someone else's hard-earned money for someone else is neither magnanimous nor intelligence. Instead, show your superiority by taking on someone's responsibility at the expense of your own hard-earned money. **Relying on others money for your happiness is foolishness.**

A self-respecting and responsible person never gets married before attaining the financial independence. But if you do so, life becomes hell. It not only destroys your self-respect but also self-confidence. You will be seen as a useless servant and get pushed towards helotism. Don't expect your partner to fulfil your personal desires, it's your job to take care of it and it's your duty to fulfil your personal aspirations. Always remember that **others should never be tortured for your extravagance, luxury, and indulgence.**

So, attain the financial independence much before you decide to get married. And never depend on your life partner to fulfil your personal desires and inner yearnings, it will not only disappoint, and frustrate you but also disappoint and frustrate your partner for sure. Instead, **self-earn for self-respect and self-earn for self-satisfaction.**

Never think of having your own children before attaining the financial freedom. Raising children comes with a hefty price tag. We often hear that buying/building a house is the biggest expense but raising children may take more than that. So, don't become a parent until you are confident that you can take care of them and their expenses yourself. **Alwaysachieve the financial independence before taking on any financial responsibilities.**

But what shall I do if I don't achieve the financial freedom even after 26? Don't lose hope. Analyse and understand, why you are not able to do it and what's stopping you? **Apply 5 WHYs on your problem statement.** This analysis helps you to understand the root cause of your problem. Once root cause is understood, you would be able to identify corrective actions. Once corrective actions are identified and taken care of, your life can start running back on track. Don't just accept your fate as it is. Try all options until you find the right one. Remember that **Your survival is your business.** And don't forget that only fittest will survive here.

But it's okey to depend on them to some extent, its ok to rely on them up to some point. but not for ever and not for everything. **It's okey to lean on someone to some extent in the worst situation, but never become an unbearable burden on anyone.**

Afterall, why it is so important and necessary? What happens if I do not achieve financial freedom? It kills your ability to move forward in life. You lose your power, you cannot make your own decisions in life, you may not be able to do what you want to do; you may not be able to try what you want to try; you may not be able to see what you want to see; you may not be able to hear what you want to hear; you may not be able to eat what you want to eat, may not able to live the way you want to live; and you may not be able to die the way you want to die. You will simply become a slave. That's why your parents were teaching you, guiding you, criticizing you and scolding you in your childhood to study well, make good friends, work hard, do your homework daily, do your exams well, be responsible, take life seriously etc., Unfortunately, those who did not understand what their parents were saying and why they were saying whatever they were saying are now suffering in life. Whoever understood are successful and leading a respectful life now.

After attaining the financial independence, usually we get busy in accumulating more and more money; we get busy in savings; we get active in making investments for our future, and we get engaged in taking loans and repaying. Of course, we get immersed in our own goals and achievements but don't forget to reserve some portion of your busy schedule for your parents and their well-being. Don't forget to set aside some portion of your income for their future needs and requirements. Be up to date on what's happening in their life and their necessities. Be there and be prepared to help them when they need your physical help, emotional support, and financial assistance.

.

What have you done for me?

.

You raised me
You praised me
You consoled me
And you surprised me

.

You liked me
You loved me
You blessed me
And you inspired me

.

You made me
You cared me
You prepared me
And you cried for me

.

You saved me
You scared me
You sheltered me
And you sacrificed for me

.

You gave birth to me
you gave life to me, but how selfish I am

how unsatisfied I am, my mind still asks me
What have you done for me? What will you do for me?

.

CHAPTER FIVE

SUCCESS

Your next gift is to promise that 'I will be successful." It is always misunderstood that, success means more money, more wealth, or more power, but it is not true unless it is your goal. Success is nothing but reaching your goal, irrespective of what the goal is. Success is advancing toward your goal with continuous progress. Yes, it's a journey, need not always be the destination. What's more important is the continuous progress with improvements. So, don't pause; never stop, let your effort continuously flow like a river until it reaches the ocean. **Bravery is not the absence of fear, but it is in the act of moving forward despite of fear.**

Success is not only about achieving goals but also about moving toward your goal with persistent effort despite of obstacles and challenges. Just set a goal and head towards it. Make progress consistently giving your best. **Don't check if I am doing better than others; check if I am doing better than what I was doing before.** It all about the positive difference that you make between yesterday and today and the difference that you are going to make between today and tomorrow.

Success is believing in yourself. It lies in your confidence, it lies in your perseverance, it is there in your focus, it is in your commitment and is in your continuous effort. If you are able to do what you would like to do, then you are successful. The most important thing is that the SUCCESS depends on is its second letter. Yes, it depends on you. So, don't overthink about failure and never worry about success too much. Let your effort, commitment and perseverance decide on it. But remember that the **Success is not final, and failure is not fatal**.

Of course, the meaning of success varies from person to person. Fame may mean success to some, but it may be recognition or awards for others; climbing the corporate ladder may mean success to one but it may be coming to power for another; making more profit or maintaining a good relationship with people may be success for few, but it may be about attaining spiritual maturity, preparing the tasty food, or making a difference in lives for few. It may mean launching a satellite for tom but winning the game may mean success to dick. It may be survival for Harry, and may be the death for someone else. So, it varies depending on the purpose or goal of one's life. By the way... **what do you mean by success? How have you defined it? Have you set your goals? If not set yet, when can you do so?**

Like any other parents, your parents too want you to succeed. They work hard to make you a successful and responsible individual in the society. They guide you; they teach you; they scold you, and they even beat you up sometimes to ensure that your walk on the path of success is firm and continuous. By the way, **do you know why do your parents want you to be successful?** because they want you to be happy. Yes. Happiness is a by-product of success, and it continuously follows success. So, you have to be successful to be happy, both success and happiness go hand in hand.

But why should I be successful? What if I don't succeed? To answer in two words, **no respect** and **no happiness**. If you are not successful, then you may have to depend on others for everything that you would like to do; you may lose your identity; your personality may get lost in the group; you may have to ask someone else's permission for everything that you would want to do; you lose your worth; you may not get what you want; you may not be able to speak what you would like to speak; you may not be able to do what you would like to do and you may not be considered seriously. **Such frustrated situations make the unsuccessful individual desperate, sad, and weak.** What about you? Do you want to be happy, and respected or not? Don't you want to be heard and considered seriously? If yes, then you have to be successful. So, decide on your gaols. What is your goal? What is the purpose of your life? And where is your plan of action? If goals are not set yet, don't wait long. Just get your goals set and proceed ahead. While setting your goals, ensure that the short term, medium term, and long-term goals are set. Advance towards it and make continuous progress. Don't wait till tomorrow to start your preparation for tomorrow's exam. Start now. Early preparation with dedication is one of the best mantras for your success. **So, today's contribution is significant for tomorrow's success. What matters is what are you doing now for your goal.** How you are using your current moment and every moment to meet your goal decides how soon success can be reached. If you can't do more, spend at least 5 mins a day on our goal. Set aside few mins of your life every day in its preparation. **Incredible success needs incredible sweat, struggle, and sacrifice.**

But isn't it difficult to achieve success?

Success is neither easy nor difficult, it just takes what it needs. But it largely depends on your preparation and dedication. It depends on how focused are you? How confident are you? How much can you sweat? how long can you struggle? How many times can you scramble? How deep can you suffer? What is your level of confidence and how dedicated are you? So, depending on your attitude, it becomes easy or difficult. But there is one simple formula for your success. What is that simple formula? **"Follow your parent's advice until you figure out your own goals and until you understand your own meaning of success."** Of course, your parent's advice may or may not take you to the zenith, but it will truly show you the right direction and move you forward on the right path. **Many times, their advice may even take you beyond your goals and beyond your definition of success too.**

Remember that, **action is the key to success.** Yes. Even 100 billion good thoughts do not equal one action. So, don't limit yourself to your thoughts, talks, and discussions but engage into action. Measure your progress because **you can't control what you can't measure.**

So, prepare yourself every day. Work hard all the time. Know that **the consistent preparation itself is a success** and will take you to new heights. Your continuous efforts will keep you up to date, it upgrades you every day and holds you ready all the time to grab any opportunity quickly that you come across and helps you to convert it into success in no time. **If you have dreams, split it into goals and take actions. Dreams without goals and actions remain dreams forever.**

If you want to be successful, learn from your experience. If you want to be successful, think positively and be self-disciplined. If you want to be successful, plan well and stick to it. If you want to be successful, show commitment and be honest. If you want to be successful, stay away from distractions and be focused. If you want to be successful, take risks and face difficulties bravely. Remember that **the greatest version of you is the disciplined version of you.**

If you want to be successful, don't be afraid of failure but take it seriously. It's okay to fail but ensure that every mistake of the previous step is well taken care of before the second step is taken forward. Although it's a journey from one stage of failure to another initially, it gives a better result in the long run. Just improve the quality of your effort between each step and come out as a better person in every attempt. Never go for second attempt without addressing the failure points of first attempt. **Failure is a good teacher, learn from it. Improve yourself and jump back into battlefield again.**

Most of the time, we do not dare to start. Risks bother us, and it scares us. But calculated risks must be taken in life to be successful. However, ensure that the risk mitigation plan is in place. **Not taking risk is one of the biggest risks** and doing nothing is obviously like accepting defeat without fight. Therefore, there is no question of success, but failure is guaranteed when you don't start what you want to achieve. **So, you must start.**

Be practical, set realistic goals, and swing into action. But don't get fascinated by the statement 'Nothing is impossible'. There are many things that are impossible for you. But if you think that something is possible, it is definitely possible for you. So, come out of your comfort zone, take first step forward, commence the process and make consistent and continuous progress.

Its okey to fail and sometimes good to fail, but never quit. Postpone the thought of quitting until you get what you want. Note that the true success lies in your effort, not in defeat. So, never surrender before failure if you truly believe in your goal. Whenever you feel like quitting, don't forget to take a step forward towards your target.

When you are in schools and colleges, have control on your thoughts, mind, and body. Be disciplined, be cultured, and observe social etiquettes. Don't get distracted and don't get over excited about opposite sex. Such infatuation and importance to physical attraction at young age will derail your journey of success.

Especially without understanding the consequences of such immature relationships, don't ask your parents to accept and approve it. When they oppose such raw love affair of early age, they appear like filmy villains and look like anti national elements. They suddenly become bad people and you start opposing them. You feel that your parents do not allow you to be happy, they are not letting you to be joyful, and they don't tolerate your independence. But they know that such immature relationships and fascinating attractions will only fool you and hurt your feelings.

If you really want to be successful, do not get into any new relationships in the name of infatuation, romance, love, or sex when you are in schools and colleges. It not only diverts your attention from your goals but also becomes the biggest hurdle. It not only destroys your primary objectives and goals but also gives an open invitation to all the unwanted problems and unnecessary troubles. This will not only divert your mind but also disturb your life. It not only creates problem for your parents but also for you and your new interest. You will slip into bigger complications without your own knowledge and lose your peace of mind. **No matter how attractive and fascinating it may seem, these unethical, and illegal relationships will ruin your future along with present.** Hence, your parents oppose such things and warn when you get indulged in such activities as it becomes big barrier in your success path.

By the way, why do your parents want you to be successful? What do they gain in your success? Instead of thinking about what parents gain by making us successful, think what you get from being successful. Because you get more than what your parents may get. After all, it's all about you, and you are the one who is going to reap the benefits of your success. **It's you who will taste the sweetness of your success and enjoy the benefits of your achievements.** So, respect their advice and strive for it.

Your parents not only just want you to be successful; not just wish you to be successful but also work behind you for your success. They applaud you when you do a good job; they encourage you to work harder; they teach you to think positively; tell success stories to inspire you and stories of failure to caution you. They guide you; advise you and do all the necessary for your success. They carve you, try hard to shape you and define the right path for you. They show you the right direction, assist you in setting up goals and help you achieving them. They encourage you; support you; motivate you and inspire you do great in life. You may remember your parents telling you not to keep complaining all the time, not to copy others, not to get involved in bad things, not to fight with your friends and siblings, etc. They tell you to come home in time, follow the culture and uphold our values. They should have advised you to exercise regularly, walk daily, study well and take care of your health to be strong, etc. **But don't let their love and care wash away in the wave of your new attractions; don't ignore their concern in the frenzy of your youth, and don't forget their sacrifice under the influence of your selfishness.**

They must have told you many times to turn off TV and do some creative work or get yourself involved in physical activities instead. They must have complained about the excessive use of cell phones or other electronic devices. They must have advised you to go to bed early in the night and get up early in the morning. They must have advised you to eat at the right time and eat well. They must have also told you to avoid junk food. They must have guided you to have more water, vegetables, and fruits for your better health. Your parents must have also told you to study hard and get a good job. They must have advised you to save money, spend less, and to have control over your wants and greed.

Your parents might have accompanied you to your schools, colleges, tuition, interviews, and workplaces. They must have advised you to behave well, speak gently and talk to others with respect. They must have guided you not to lie, not to cheat and not to deceive others. They must also have advised you to be calm, cool, and not to get angry. They must have guided you to choose your friends carefully, be with good people, do good work and avoid bad company. They must also have warned you on you bad behaviour and might have scolded you on your faults and habits.

If you talk to any successful person, they talk about their parents' contribution in their success. They talk about their parents' sacrifice, advice, and guidance behind their success story. Remember that your success is not just yours; there are four more hands, four more legs and two more heads. Don't forget that there are two more hearts which constantly beat for you and pray for your success.

When you promise your parents about your success, look for overall success and strive for complete success. Believe in your hard work, your strength, and your power rather others for your success. Now a days, most of the people around us think that economic success is the real success and is the complete success. Of course, the economic success is very important. Without which, people don't treat us like people. therefore, economic success is very significant in today's money driven world but not sufficient for your overall success. Along with economic success, one should also achieve physical success, mental success, family success, social success, recreational success, and spiritual success.

Physical success is the success in maintaining good physical health. It helps you to be healthy and live longer. Set physical health goals for your physical well-being and achieve it without fail. **If you look after your body, it looks after you. If you respect your body, it respects you. If you care your body, it cares you.** Mental success is the success in mental health. It is a discovery of peace within oneself. Set your goals related to mental health and achieve it for your mental well-being. It helps people to be happy and peaceful throughout their life. **It doesn't mind If you take care of your mind, instead it likes you and takes care of your peace of mind.**

Family success is the success of the family. Our family includes the most beloved, important, and precious people of our life. It is difficult for anyone to be happy when their family is suffering. So, ensure that you family members are not suffering from bad health, financial problems, or mental anguishes. How can one be successful when his family or a member of family has failed? So, work for your family and ensure that everything is okay and all is well in the family.

Social success is the success of your society. Human beings are social animals. They want to stay connected with people. They want to be known, they want to be praised, they want to be respected, they want to be appreciated, and they want to get related with other people in the society. Like our family, our society also includes people who matter to us in our day-to-day life. How can one be happy in a sick society and how can one be joyful in between bad people? How will you celebrate your success in a failed society? So, work for your society and its upliftment. Work for its health and its well-being. And try to do better for others. **Those who work for society, society works for them.** So, contribute in building a better society.

Fun and entertainment are very important in everyone's life. Set your entertainment goals and plan well for its execution. It's important to have excitement and entertainment in life. So, plan recreational activities at regular intervals and achieve the recreational success without a miss.

Spiritual success is about understanding who I am. It is about establishing a link between you and your god. Strengthening your connection with universe and its Spirit. When you know who you are, you can be truly who you are. **It's about understanding the real purpose of your birth and figuring out the actual reasons to live till the death.** Wake up to your real life and understand the real purpose.

As said earlier, when you promise to be successful, then look for overall success, and look for complete success.

Being successful in one area and failing in another does not make you a complete. **So, always strive for complete success.** Build your own fort and rule your life in your own style king size.

.

Successful ?

.

I studied well, I got the job
I am earning well now
But I did not care them
I did not respect them
And did not help them
Am I Successful?

.

I am grown up, I got married
I have a spouse and children now
But I did not support my parents
I did not make them happy
and left them all alone
Am I Successful?

.

I worked hard, I run my business
I have made enough money and wealth now
But I did not live with my parents in their last days
I did not worry about their necessities
And brought tears in their eyes
Am I Successful?

.

I struggled, I achieved.
I have a name now. I have fame now
But I did not solve any of my parents' problems
I did not walk with them in their pain
And did not repay their loan

Am I Successful?

.

CHAPTER SIX

Don't leave. Live

It has been seen that young children are running away from homes. May be because of fear, anger, or insult. They are absconding because of the stress, conflict, or strain. Though it is a foolish fleeting reaction of immature intellect, its impact and stigma endure. It is not only immature, foolish, and filthy but also a sin and nothing more than that of a betrayal and treachery. So, gift them a promise that 'Í don't leave home but live with my parents'.

Furthermore, running away from home is extremely dangerous, life-threatening, and fatal. This kind of stupidity can destroy your present and decay your future. You will not only lose your present love, care, and comfort, but also the future. You will not only get exposed to unseen cruel world but also become a dumb victim of your own decision with nobody to blame. You may run away for your freedom, but this decision can put you in cage forever.

You would not only regret but also remorse. World not only laughs at you but also make fun of you. It makes you stand naked in front of it and will burn you alive. Hence, stay away from such meaningless thoughts and immature acts. When you decide to run, remember that no one assures you freedom and there is no guarantee of return.

There is a big difference between 'Thinking about running away' and 'Actually running away'. Outside world is crueller than that of you think. There will be more restrictions, more rules, more stress, and more fights than at home. Struggle begins for the basics. The ride of brutality begins, and cruelty starts. You will have no food to eat, no place to sleep, no people to care and no money to spend. But you will find many to insult, hurt and exploit you. Runaway kids engage in dangerous crimes and may get vulnerable to assault, rapes, and murder. They start stealing to meet basic needs and many start drugs and alcohol too. No one cares about them and get exposed to deadly diseases on roads.

Runaways show an increased risk general health problems and emotional disorders, such as anxiety, depression, and suicide attempts. Living alone outside at young age exposes you to outrage, abuse, molest, attack, sexual assault, and diseases. You may even get exposed to threats and murders. Many teens who run away end up in smuggling, drug-dealing, human trafficking, prostitution, underworld operations and other illegal activities for food and a place to stay.

Instead of running away, express your emotions and explain your parents how you are feeling inside. Get some help from trusted adults if you are not comfortable with your parents. Reach out to your grandparents, teachers, good friends, a close relative, or any one you trust can help you. But never run away from home. Most of the children end up working in shops, hotels, and homes as slaves. They indulge in begging and suffer whole life in bad hands.

WHERE ARE YOU?

Don't go alone; Don't go far
Don't leave home; return in time
She waits, He calls
Where are you?
When are you coming?

.

Don't walk the wrong path.
don't take wrong decision; Don't run away.
She waits, He calls
Where are you?
When are you coming?

.

Their nights are long; days are dark
Face is withered; eyes are dried
She is waiting, He is calling
Where are you?
When are you coming?

.

Their breath is hot; Blood is clot
Heart is full; and they are unwell
She is waiting, He is calling
Where are you?
When are you coming?

.

Their thoughts are bad; Mind going mad
life getting hard; and are thinking wild
She is waiting, He is calling
Where are you?
When are you coming?

.

It has also been noticed that young children not only think about suicide but also go to the extent of committing suicide due to fear, failure, insult, and stress or of their own reasons. Though it's a hot-headed reaction by an innocent mind in a vulnerable state, the consequences, shame, and stigma will haunt for a long time. You may think that you would get free from all your problems and issues, but what is the use of such freedom in death? Stay away from such meaningless thoughts, don't even think of such heinous acts. Always remember that your life is not just yours. It also belongs to your parents. Not just your parents, but also to nature, nation, mother earth, and the almighty god. It belongs to all those who are directly and indirectly responsible for your birth and growth. So, it's mandatory to get their permission and approval before you decide to take your life. You can't end it without their consent and can never destroy it without their approval. Instead, take charge of your life, face your problem, fix it, and finish it. **Solve the problem before it dissolves you; kill the problem before it kills you.** Remember that **living your life is your birth right and an act of courage.**

Don't take axe to cut the plant shoot. **Finding permanent solution to a temporary problem is not always a wise decision.** Don't go to the extent of declaring a war against your body. Don't think of killing an emotionally weak person (yourself). No bravery in defeating a defeated man. Just because, it's your own body, you can't hurt it. Just because it's your own life, you can't end it. There may not be an outside slayer in suicide, but killer is there for sure. Don't be your murderer. Don't become a victim of your own plot. No matter how cruel the situation is, no matter how big the problem is and no matter how difficult your difficulty may be. Bear and endure until you find the solution. It's just a phase in your life; it's just a step in your journey, it's just a turn in your path; it's just a chapter in your book, move on and move forward. **Your problem can't be your destination. Its just a bad time; take rest; it will pass. Its just a bad weather; give time; it will change. Its just a wind; stay strong and hold tight; Normalcy will return. Nothing is permanent here. Neither sadness nor happiness; neither grief nor joy. Our life is mixture of all; it keeps taking turns. Respect this game and enjoy it at the same time.**

We know that everyone dies, and no one is immortal here. We clearly understand the hard truth that **we come together only to get separate.** We know that our **loved ones will leave us, and we leave them.** There is no Mistry here. Being an intelligent species among the living beings, we all understand that **we have born to die**, we have come to go, **we have gathered to separate,** and **we laugh to cry.** But the only thing that we do not know is "**when.**" As per the rule of nature, whatever takes birth should meet death, whatever starts should end, and whatever comes should go. So, don't hurt your body and don't hurt your soul. Whether you want or not, you have to go one day. Don't be in a hurry. God can never acknowledge, he will never accept, and will never approve such a heinous act. Instead, be in the game and face the situation even if you are sure of failure. Turns of life will change the conditions and conditions will change positions. Time changes situations and new situations create new opportunities. So, your turn will come, your time will come, and new opportunities will give you better life. So, don't shut the door; don't close the window, let the fresh air come in, let the sun light kiss you. There may be temporary setback while playing but never admit your defeat until your game is over. Remember that

God can give only chances in life but not a new life again.

The harshest and cruellest punishment one can give to their parents is suicide. Your weak mind may think that suicide may be the panacea, but it's nothing but a dirty, filthy, immature momentary mistake. In fact, the act of committing suicide is a clear-cut betrayal of trust, love, care, respect, and dignity of yourself, your parents, and your family. It's a treachery shown to God. **Your parents can forgive you if you kill them, but they can never forgive you if you kill yourself.** By killing yourself, you not only kill yourself but also kill their love, respect, care, perseverance, strength, dignity, laughter, and the rest of their life.

Never think that they cannot help you; never think that they cannot pull you through. Don't think that they don't forgive you and not ever believe that they hate you. Not even once think that they do not love you; On no occasion believe that they do not like you, and don't ever assume that they leave your hand. Have full faith and confidence that, they will do anything and everything for you when such a situation arises. Don't jump to any conclusion when you are disappointed with them. And never decide anything when you are angry on them. **Such hasty conclusions and decisions can lead to major accidents.**

The best way to handle your weak moment when suicidal thoughts are provoking and instigating you for suicide is **"not to act but to wait."** In fact, **'Waiting' is a very powerful mantra.** It helps in many ways. When you are about to start something wrong, cruel, and wicked, wait; when you are about to start something you think should not be done, wait; When you are about to start something which your heart and mind is denying, wait; when you are about to hit someone in angry, wait, and when you are about scold someone, wait. Just wait for some time.It stabilizesyour mind; controls your emotions and diverts your attention. **Wait before you burst, wait before you hurt, wait before you bark in angry and wait before you do any heinous act.** Patience calms you down; it brings you back to normal; it gives opportunity to think what is right and what is wrong and helps you to take prudent decision.

When you are about to make such known mistake or any mistake, don't act but wait. Check if God has approved to proceed ahead or not. If God has not agreed yet, then wait; he may be busy at the moment. Wait for some more time, if no response, then go out for a cup of coffee or tea and come back. But wait until he gives green signal. If it is getting delayed further, call your parents, or loved ones and talk to them. Put your problems and difficulties in front of them like a small child. It helps and can give you the 2nd life before your first death. But wait! Don't act until God's approval is in place.

Research says that parents who lose their child to suicide are at high risk of mental health problems. They are prone to developing severe depression and anxiety disorders. The grief associated with suicide is very complex and severe compared with other causes of death. The level of depression and mental disorders is significantly higher among parents whose children have committed suicide. They keep mourning for the rest of their life. **You may die on that day, but they keep on dying every day after that day.**

After they lose their child to suicide, their perception of life may change. Things that were very important earlier may not mean anything after that, same thoughts keep coming and start killing them mentally. Same questions but no answers ... why did this happen to us? Where did we fail? What blunder did we make? What went wrong? What was our fault? How we could have avoided? What we would have done differently? And many more one after the other. Of course, the answer may serve no purpose, but questions continue to strike one after the other without pause. Every boy or a girl that they see reminds them of their lost son or daughter. Their intense sorrow is indescribable. Their grief is unimaginable. They feel like screaming loudly. They feel like scratching tightly. No one can console them, and nothing can calm them down. The irony is that whoever can console them or calm them down is no longer with them. They keep blaming and pinning themselves all the time. Every day becomes a nightmare, and every moment becomes stressful. Day gets long, and the night goes sleepless. Tears get dried out, and blood gets clotted. Don't leave them; live with them. Don't leave them; be with them.

Such problems with unbearable pain and pressure debilitates! On top of it, our inability to handle such situation makes us vulnerable. In such vulnerable moments, the mind wanders and provokes weirdness. But instead of surrendering to a weak mind, one should ask oneself **is the current situation a challenge or a problem.?** Most of the people get confused between problem and challenge and think that their challenges are their problems. **But challenge is not a problem, It's just a demanding task or a situation.**

Most of the time, most of the people would be in challenging situations, not in a vortex of unsolvable problems. Challenge is something new or a difficult job which requires extra effort and determination. It can be overcome with hard work, intelligence, and guidance. Whereas Problem is something difficult to understand or deal with. It's a situation which hinders the progress but can be solved. So, Gauge the situation accurately and decide wisely whether you are in a problem or in a challenging situation? **If you can't handle the situation, handle yourself. And if you can't control the situation, control your reaction.**

If you are in a challenging situation, you can overcome with your hard work, intelligence, and guidance. If you're in a problem, find solution. We should try to find the solution rather than going in isolation. The best approach when you are in deep problem or depression is to discuss about it with someone close to your heart. Having open conversations about any problems or suicidal thoughts may help alleviate a pain. Most of the cases, it's our immaturity and ignorance which provokes us to go up to that extent but not the actual problem or pressure. Always keep in mind **if you have created a problem, you can solve it. If someone else has created, it can definitely be delt with. But if God has created, he will help you for sure.** So, **Live, believe and be alive.**

If you think anxiety, bipolar disorder, depression, schizophrenia, or any other mental disorder is a valid reason for committing suicide, then you are wrong. This is not a valid reason for suicide, but it's a challenge and a valid reason to prove to yourself and to the entire world that you are not weak but a fighter and a great warrior. You must swim until you find space to stand. You may feel that the entire world is against you, every person on the planet is opposing you, and the whole nature is conspiring on you, every living being laughs at you, but believe that your parents stand with you. Control yourself, mend your mind, bring it back on track, come out of your assumption and illusions, educate your mind, guide it, and show the right direction with the help of your parents and doctors. If you cannot talk to people, then talk to nature. It will guide you. Put in an honest effort to come out of it. Find out what your interests are, what makes you happy, cool, and calm, what makes you feel free and normal, and do what gives you strength and happiness. Important thing is **don't sit idle but get busy.** Remember that no problem is bigger than you. **Bravery is not the absence of fear, but it is in the act of moving forward despite of fear.**

Shocking, disturbing, and traumatic experiences in life can sometimes lead you to suicidal thoughts. It's not your mistake. There is no fault in you. and you are not responsible for such bad incidents and worst experiences. If you find yourself responsible for any such mistakes or incidents, then correct them, but do not become a victim of someone else's mistake. Fight against it, fight against the culprit, and fight against your thought of suicide. Never murder a good person in you.

Sometimes, a few sensitive and smooth minds take bullying very seriously. Never give more importance to anyone or anything than required; do not endure but protest; do not encourage but end. If you cannot handle this, please take the help from others. Parents, siblings, friends, relatives, the police, society, nature, God, or take the help of whoever you believe in. Or just slap tight whoever is troubling you instead of slapping your parents through suicide.

Unemployment bothers. But not a serious life-threatening problem. There are many ways. You have many options to live on. Do not think about a small or big. Try what you get or do what you know. **Remember that everything big started small.**

If loneliness is creating problems for you, then get into new activities, new relationships, go to new places, join new courses, and do new things. Learn something new. Try and do something not done before. This keeps you busy; gives you challenge and makes your life interesting. It can also give new companions to walk together.

Sometimes, a bad relationship could create major problems in life. Try to correct it, work hard to bring it back on track, make sacrifices, burry your ego, nullify your expectations, give more time, spend some money, do whatever you think helps to improve your relationship. If you think that the relationship is more important, then it's okay to surrender but not all the time. The most important thing in a relationship is to lose and let your partner win. Take time, be patient, console yourself, work on you, correct yourself, keep yourself calm, test your patience, and increase your level of endurance. If nothing works out, don't be the sole victim of harassment for a long time. If you do not have any hopes that it will be fine one day, then come out of it. But spend enough time (at least 20-25% of the total time that you have spent with that person so far) to recondition your relationship. For example, if you have been in a relationship with someone for ten years, you should spend at least two to two and half years getting your relationship back on track. If you have been in a relationship for less than 5 years, you should give yourself one to one and half years before ending it. But never think of suicide. This world is overpopulated and full of people. You will find someone better to start afresh.

Financial difficulties can bother and take you to any mental state. First, look for help from yourself, your parents, friends, relatives, and banks. If it does not work out, sell your property, gold, or whatever you have. If it is not sufficient, go and request lender, borrow time. If nothing works out, surrender to him, seek his advice, discuss, reconcile, and ask for a settlement. But never think of suicide. **New opportunities will help you; good time will support you and fresh air will give you fresh life if you stay alive.** Be patient, do wait and keep doing what is necessary until you come out of your problem.

Exams, love, or business failures are another set of foolish reasons for committing suicide. Never, ever commit suicide because of an exam failure. Education is completely different from intelligence. An uneducated individual can be more intelligent, smarter, and brighter than an educated. It has nothing to do with life. A dropout's life can get better and brighter than that of an educated person. So, never think that the failure in study is a disaster or catastrophe. **There is a way for sure if you have the will.**

A failure of love should never be taken seriously. It's not at all a reason for suicide. Don't hurt yourself for someone. You will always get a better one. Remember that **failure always reminds you that you need to do it better.** Remember that theworld is overpopulated and full of peoplc. You will always find someone better to start afresh.

Suicidal thoughts can never help you but can destroy you and those who love you. Instead, seek help. Please let someone close to you know about your thoughts. Someone or the other can help you only when your thought and problems are shared with them. Never keep your suicidal thoughts a secrete, share it with your well-wishers and listen to them. **Always remember that you are not alone as long as your parents are alive** and do not quit the battlefield so easily. A thought of suicide can only come when a weak mind and a lazy body sit at one place and do nothing other than think about it. **The only way out at that point of time is to talk to someone you love the most or go to hospital and meet doctor or call suicide** helpline number or go for a long walk or go out to eat your favourite food or drive your body to some good place, may be a Divine one.

Sincere and serious advice is "Do discuss before you decide". Do listen; listening helps and acts as a saviour. No matter how dark tonight is, tomorrow dawns. Your emotions are not permanent, and situations are not stagnant. Wait, don't act. We don't know what lies ahead. Give life a chance to surprise. And always remind yourself that you matter and your existence matters, you are important, and your existence is important.

.

DON'T DIE

.

Don't die don't die
Never ever try
Don't die don't die
Until call comes from the sky

.

Think right, do right
Always be straight
Get sweat, put effort
Keep pulling the cart

.

Don't stop don't halt
Don't ever take a break
keep pulling Keep pushing
Never apply the break

.

Keep moving Keep running
Never ever cry

Keep struggling keep fighting
Never ever die

.

Keep talking, keep listening
Don't stop walking
Keep swimming, keep moving
Never stop breathing

.

Stay strong, stay happy
Let the whole world wonder
How can you still be happy
And how can you still be so strong

.

Don't shy don't die
Never ever try
Don't die don't cry
Until call comes from the sky

.

CHAPTER SEVEN

SUPPORT

It is important to be good and surround ourselves with good people. Because, we all need others support and at the same time we must also need to support others. So, being good and having good people around us is important. Such people give confidence, give hope, and boost our energy. Their genuine encouragement, reassurance, and compassion strengthen us and bring new light to our life. They not only enhance the quality of our life but also come to our rescue during adverse life events. They influence us positively and are important for our physical and mental well-being. So, don't lose such people and never lose their trust. Always keep your relationship, friendship and your association with such people securely. Because they are valuable.

Fortunately, we are surrounded by such people by default at home - our parents. They stay with us and help us from the first day of our birth. They keep supporting us in one or the other way throughout their life. They help us in our difficult time and extend their support all the time. **But we rarely ask whether they need our support.** We think that our parents are here only to support us, and we are here to enjoy their support. We feel that it is their duty to support us, and we expect them to do their duty without any mistakes. But we usually forget to enquire about their well-being. They also need our support and help. Yes. Your next gift is to promise that "I support my parents". **Assure that you are there for them.**

Support them in day-to-day work. Keep your study books, bags, and table in order. Sort your shoes and place them in their shelf nicely. Keep your house clean and tidy. Bring ration, groceries, and necessaries home. Help in food preparation. Clean the table, carry plates, and wash them after meal. Assist them in their business and help them in their farming. Join hands in their challenges and support them in their need.

They not only support you but also sacrifice for you. After becoming parents, they don't just remain husband and wife but become your mom and dad. **Once they become your father and mother, their journey of sacrifice begins and continues till their end.** They lose their time and They lose their privacy. Relaxing after a busy day of work becomes challenging and a deep sleep without disturbance becomes a matter of luxury for years. They lose their freedom; they rarely get free time, and peace of mind becomes a thing of the past. Even then, they show us unconditional love and teach us the true meaning of selflessness.

They spend their hard-earned money to fulfil their kid's needs and spend their well-earned money to satisfy their wants. They even go beyond their limitations for your better opportunities. Their relationship with their spouse gets affected after your birth and takes a hit during your growth. Their social life takes back seat and their wish list find place in the dust bin. Their professional life too takes hit. But they neither regret nor remorse.

So, don't doubt their commitment just because they are teaching you what is right and what is wrong. Don't get upset just because they guide you how to behave and how not; don't question their love just because they ask you to be responsible; don't lose your trust just because they don't allow you to do what you would like to do. Their purpose is to prepare you for tomorrow. Their objective is to equip you to be confident to face the world boldly. Their intention is to bring it to your attention that the life isn't always a bed of roses, but also contains thorn. All that they want you to understand is "**Life is a responsibility, not just a right.**"

So, don't take them wrong and never forget their support. At the same time, ensure that they get your support when they are in need of it. But do you know, how you can support your parents? They are many ways... Support your parents showing your respect. It's very important for them to see how they are getting treated by their own blood in front of the world. Basically, how you treat your parents in public; how you care them in front of others; how you behave with them when people are around; how you speak and how much attention you pay to their needs and wants is what matters. How do you feel when someone shouts at you in front of others? **If we can speak gently with our friends, neighbours, colleagues and relatives, why can't with our own parents?** How you feel if your teacher or boss scolds you in front of everyone? How you feel when your parents yell at you in front of your friends or relatives? Obviously, you get offended and feel insulted. Isn't it? At the same time, how do you feel when someone recognizes, appreciates, or respects you in front of others? Happy, proud, and honoured? Yes. How we are treated by someone and how we treat someone especially in front of others matters a lot. So, choose your words carefully when you are talking to them in front of their friends and relatives. **If you treat people for what they are, they remain what they are. But if you treat them better, they get better.**

When you praise them in front of their own people, they feel respected. When you touch their feet in presence of others, they feel honoured, and they may feel reverent when you do it in private. **If you respect them, others will also respect them but if you neglect, others will insult them.** So, always respect your parents. Your children and spouse will learn from you and will follow the same culture. **How you treat others tells what you are; how others treat you tells who you are!**

Never snatch their financial freedom by asking them for money in their old age. Let them spend their earnings the way they want to and allow them to lead their life the way they would like to. Instead, extend your economic support to them if needed. Reserve a portion of your income for their future needs and well-being. Perhaps you can **set aside around 15-20% of your monthly income for their necessities regardless of whether they need your financial assistance or not. but setting aside a portion of your income for their needs and necessities is your responsibility.** Its good if it comes to their help in their need, if not, use it for your needs or for your children's future after their demise. But it is always essential to reserve and manage good amount of money for their needs as a reserve fund or provident fund.

Being children, we always expect them to do their duties towards us properly. And find flaws in whatever they do. But have you ever questioned yourself about your duties towards them? What are you doing for your parents' fun, enjoyment and happiness? We assume that they are old now and are not interested in fun and entertainment. But you may be wrong. Ask them, **"Who is your favourite hero or heroine?"** Take them to movies. Enquire about their interests, take them to plays, musical performances, fun worlds, water games, sporting events, family functions, foreign trips, and to their favourite places. Make a list of their loved ones [friends, relatives, colleagues, walk mates, classmates, anyone who they would like to see, talk with, and spend some time with] and take them to their homes and places.

You can support them by not spoiling their name, it is significant to them; Don't ruin their dignity in family or in society, it is important to them; Don't tarnish their reputation and don't damage their respect in the society, it is substantial to them. **Never make them walk their heads down instead save their hard-earned reputation, uplift their respect, enhance their dignity, and make them feel proud in the society.**

Look after your parents in their poor health. Usually, children do not pay much attention to their parents' minor health issues like headache, toothache, back pain, knee pain, diabetes, high blood pressure (BP), low blood pressure, etc., but these small health problems make their life irritating, frustrating, vexing, and bothersome in their old age. Your solace and support make them feel better. Stand by their side while they are resting on hospital bed, it gives them physical comfort and mental peace. Prepare a cup of hot coffee and serve them while they are suffering from headache; press their tired feet after their long walk and give them a head massage when they feel stressed and tired. Your health tips can make them feel better and your suggestions could work like medicines. Your support can act like a treatment and your care can bring their strength back to life.

We are all living in an innovation era. Every day, new gadgets, new apps, new instruments, new tools, new foods, new vehicles, and new businesses are being introduced and launched in the market. This 'new' has become a part of our day-to-day life and this 'newness' doesn't stay new for a long time; it becomes old soon; its validity has come down drastically nowadays. Adjusting ourselves to these new things has become an inevitable part of our daily life. Hence, we need to keep upgrading ourselves and our parents with the latest innovations and technologies around. Since "newness" has become new normal, you should take time to teach them how to use or operate any new tool, app, or instruments. Often, children seen saying, **"How many times do I need to tell you this?", "I cannot repeat it anymore!", "Every time, I should start from the beginning." "You don't know this much!".** Don't lose your patience, have tolerance; upgrade them calmly, guide them slowly, and bring them up to speed on current events and innovations gently.

Don't think that they are too old to try something new. **Never decide that they are aged enough to try anything new**; It should always be left to their decision; let them make that decision depending on their interest, strengths, and weaknesses. Your job is to encourage them to try new things in life. Motivate them to join a painting class or an English-speaking course; stimulate them to go to a musical class or a computer course; drive them to go and meet their old friends and prompt them for yoga classes. Urge them for cycling, dancing, playing games, sports, joining a theatre groups, photography or cookery classes. Push them for writing poems, reading new books, and attending social functions. Encourage them for gardening, travelling and hobbies. Inspire them for social service and help them in do something or the other that makes them feel like they are learning and enjoying the current phase of their life.

Are you aware of your parents' goals and objectives? Have you ever asked your parents what their short-term and long-term goals are? They spend more than 50% of their life making sure your goals are met. They even go the extra mile by sacrificing their own ambitions and aspirations. They let go their own aims for the sake of their children's aims and intentions. Therefore, it is important for you to be aware of their goals and aspirations in order to support them meeting their goals and fulfilling their aspirations.

Support them physically, support them mentally, support them financially and support them spiritually. Support in their poor health; support in their difficult time; support in their old age, and support in their last stage. Know their requirements; understand their needs; meet their expectations and manage their emotions. Don't ignore their torn cloths, don't neglect their torn slipper, and don't overlook their broken eyeglasses. Don't make them feel bad; don't make them feel sad; don't let them suffer and don't give them trouble.

When you are grown up and get too busy, find time to talk to them, find time to walk with them. Talk to them at least for 10 to 15 minutes a day; walk with them at least for 100 mins a week. They don't just listen to your words; they experience the love, care, and affection behind your talks. Such conversations energise them. And such discussions give them the freshness. Your presence gives them the courage and your stay with them gives satisfaction. Your support makes them stronger, and your voice gives them the energy. Therefore, get along with them, especially when you are in your teenage and when they are in their old age.

Most importantly, know their problems, troubles, and difficulties. Understand their dilemma, challenges, obstacles, and worries. Be with them in their troubles; stand with them in their challenges and work with them in their difficulties. Assure that you will solve their problems and get rid of their worries.

Your verbal assurance that 'I am here for your support' itself can do wonders; it has immense potential. The sound of your words that 'I am here for you' has every potential to give them the courage and mental peace. Such reassurance not only gives them emotional support but also solves up to 50% of their problems. Simply being around them during their difficult time brings them a big relief and great comfort. But don't just assure and sit on your verbal assurance, spring into action to solve the remaining 50% of their problems.

They were there at every stage of our life, and we were taken complete care of up to a certain age of our life. They were there with their words of wisdom when we were down in the dumps. They were there with their helping hands when we were sink in sump. They were there with their guidance when we were in trouble, and they were there with their solution when we were in problem. They were there to lift us up when we were down. And they were there to wake us up when we were asleep. There were there when we needed them, and they were there when we wanted their support. But everything comes to an end. Their health may not allow them; their age may not permit them, and their stage may not support them to keep supporting us. It is hard after creatin age and difficult after certain stage.

Of course, they sacrifice a lot for us, for our happiness and for our well-being. Their sacrifice starts from the 1st day of our birth and continues till the last day of their death. They keep working for us in one or the other way. **Parents never take retirement. But give them a break and let them take rest.** Show your care, genuine love and be there to support them.

In some cases, the relationships between children and parents breaks down after marriage. The flower of a relationship starts withering when your importance starts slowly swinging between parents and spouse. At this point, your relationship with your parents needs additional support. Make it strong with your constant love and extra effort. It is true that the new members of the family should also be given importance and significance, but it can slightly be lower than that of your parents'. Because of their age, stage, sacrifice, and unconditional love that they have showered on you since your birth. **Support your parents openly and convince your spouse privately.** Never allow any new relationships to come between you and your parents. And at the same time, never allow anybody to come between the relationship of you and your spouse. **This is a sensitive issue; handle it with care and intelligence.**

Never be the source of a problem. If possible, be part of the solution. The main reason why parents are facing health issues in their early stage is due to family problems and the unbearable stress in their personal life. **Your parents should feel happy, healthy, and proud because you are there in the family, but not because you are not.** Looks like children are directly responsible for minimum 20 percent of their parent's problems, worries and health issues. How about you? **How much is your contribution in your parents' health and happiness? And what is your role in your parents' ill-health and worries?Never become their problem or source of their worries but be a ray of hope and their hope of solutions.**

.

Its Okey, but...

.

Its okey if you don't support
Its ok if you can't support
But don't hurt and never ill-treat

.

She has given birth to you, he has given life to you
And they have given love to you
Support them and stay with them in their need

.

Be with them in their troubles
Work with them in their difficulties
And stand firm along with them in their challenges

.

Serve them, they have served you enough
Help them, they have helped you enough
Work for them, they have sweated it out for you

.

Don't become their problem
Never become an unanswerable question
Help them in their old age and stay with them in their
last stage

.

When road is long, winds of the life are strong
When hope is gone, feel like can't go on

Their support comes as your beacon

.

Be there and stand with them in their need
Support them physically, support them emotionally
support them financially and spiritually

.

Be there and stand with them in their need
Its okey if you don't support, its ok if you can't support
But don't hurt and never ill-treat

.

CHAPTER EIGHT

HELP

Your next gift is to promise that "I help my parents" Help is nothing but making someone feel at ease, relaxed and comfortable by offering our service or resources. Do you agree that your parents offered their service and resources to make your life easier and comfortable? Yes. They help us in all the possible ways throughout their life. In fact, the first 30-40% of our life is completely dependent on the mercy, sacrifice, help, and support of our parents.

They don't just help and support us. They don't just perform their duties and responsibilities; they go beyond that. They have not only helped you but also served you. They have not just raised you but also loved you. They have not just consoled you but also cared you. They have not just educated you but also disciplined you. They have not just blessed you but also protected you. They have not just sheltered you but also educated you. They have not only discouraged you but also motivated you. They have not only guided you but also tested you. They have not only challenged you but also comforted you. They have not only corrected you but also prepared you. They have not only influenced you but also inspired you. They have not only praised you but also advised you. They have not only given you freedom but also restricted you. They have not only cried for you but also worked for you. They have not only played with you but also prayed for you. They have not only sheltered you but also sacrificed for you. They have not only helped you but also served you. They held you in their hands when your legs pained. They put you to sleep when you dozed, and they understood you before it is said.

They laughed when you laughed. They cried when you cried. They walked when you walked, and they talked when you talked. They ran when you ran. They enjoyed when you enjoyed; They got afraid when you were afraid, they got tensed when you were tensed. They got scared when you came home late, and they were worried when you didn't answer their phone calls.

They not only help us in every step of our life, but also support us in every stage of our life. They not only help us but also care us; they not only love us but also listen to us. But what are we doing for them? Isn't it our duty to help them when they need help? Isn't it our responsibility to help them when they can't help themselves? Isn't it our obligation to support them when they need other's support? Yes, we must help them at different points of our life and at the different stages of their life.

But do we know how we can help our parents at different points of our life and how can we help them at different stages of their lives?

Help by spending their money cautiously. Be cautious while spending their sweat drops and be thoughtful while flowing out their hard-earned money for your transient enjoyment and temporary entertainment. Understand the fact that they may not be able to afford all your wants and wishes and may not be able to fulfil all your desires and demands. **Their duty is to provide you what is necessary, but not luxury and lavishness.** Reduce your expenses on unwanted and unnecessary things and shun the habit of enjoying luxury in others money. Of course, whatever is unnecessary or unwanted for others may be necessary for you. but don't blow out their money lavishly and don't bother them just to flaunt false richness. **If you are draining it out for your show off, then waste it with some shyness and embarrassment.**

Choose good people, understand their nature, measure their value, and weigh their worth and then choose the right one as your friend. Good friends are not only warm-hearted but also witty; they are not only understanding but also unconditional; they are not only truthful but also trustworthy; they are not only sympathetic but also supportive; they are not only straight-froward but also sincere; they are not only receptive but also reliable; they are not only practical but also protective; they are not only positive but also playful; they are not only observant but also optimistic; they are not only motivational but also non-judgemental; they are not only lovable but also loyal; they are not only intuitive but inspirational; they are not only genuine but also grateful; they are not only faithful but also fearless; they are not only energetic but also enthusiastic; they are not only empathetic but also encouraging; They encourage you to keep going even it is tough and inspire you to succeed even when it is difficult. Good friends not only encourage healthy behaviour but also give their shoulder. They not only give you emotional support but also bring humour to life. Spending time with good friends reduce stress and anxiety. They teach you; they challenge you; they motivate you; they inspire you; they support you; they love you; they trust you, and they help you. But bad friends not only spoil your present but also make your future miserable. Even though their association makes your present pleasurable but long-term connection will destroy the future.

You can help your parents by staying away from bad habits. Bad habits interrupt the growth and prevent us from accomplishing goals. It jeopardizes our health, wastes our time and kills our energy. Though you feel that the bad habits are good for present pleasure, it ruins your future choices. Though it gives transient happiness but brings perpetual sadness. A bad habit not only makes you bad but also kills the good in you. Therefore, stay away from bad habits and be far away from bad people but embrace good habits and never loose good people. **If it is difficult to break bad habit, replace it with good.**

You can help them by not getting into new relationships at young age especially during your studies. Young and immature mind may not be able to handle all the emotions and pains of such affairs. And such relations may lead to personal disaster. You will not only lose your good friends and family members but also get deviated from your mainstream. It becomes difficult to find the balance and gets tough to manage disapproving parents. It not only results in poor performance in studies but may lead to delinquency. Although present looks pleasant and beautiful, future will be ugly.

Never hide your problems but share with your parents. Especially when you are young and in teenage, don't play hide and seek with your parents. Help them by discussing about your problems, troubles, struggles and feelings openly. Help them by having open discussions on all your issues and difficulties. Help them by not struggling all alone in yourself. Seek their opinions, suggestions, and guidance for your problems.

You can help them riding your vehicles carefully. Drive to return home safe. Vehicle accidents are real and sometimes unavoidable. Even minor accidents that cause no injury can have negative and long-lasting effects. Think of financial loss, potential lawsuits, road disruptions, long-lasting traumas, phobias, and anxiety associated with rash driving and accidents. Therefore, be careful while driving. It is not only those physically involved in the accident who are affected but it also affects their families, friends, and passer-by's. **Though the speed thrills, it kills.** Each year, 1.35 million people are killed on roadways around the world. Every day, almost 3,700 people are killed globally in road accidents. It means, more than two persons are getting killed every minute. **In fact, speed does not kill people, but sudden immobility does.** So, drive to save, not to kill. And drive to live, not to die.

You can help by being grateful. They spend 2nd half of their whole life grooming, programming, raising, supporting, and helping you. They are the only people on earth you can trust closing your eyes. They don't speak negatively about you; they listen to your side of the story and defend you. They help you and protect you. They forgive your mistakes and forget your faults. They give you chances and help you overcome your problems. Help them by not blaming them for your failure.

You can help them understanding their pain and feelings. You can help them by being supportive and sympathetic about their grievances. You can help them by maintaining a good relationship with your siblings and relatives, you can help your parents through your growth and development. You can help them by helping yourself with good health, wealth, and happiness.

Help them in hardship of their life. Help them by being part of their difficulties. Help them by understanding their concerns and anxieties. Help them understanding their emotions and feelings. Discuss openly on their issues and concerns as well. Get involved in finding solution to their problems and give them your suggestions.

You can help your father by taking care of your mother. And you can help your mother by taking care of your father. They would like to see the love and respect for their partner in your eyes. You can help by being with them during their difficult days. And you can also help them being part of their grievance. You can help them by taking them out for a movie, dinner, trip, tour, and for prayer as and when needed. If your parents are ill, be around them. take care of them. Take them to the hospital; get the treatment done; understand the course of medicine and medicate them accordingly.

You can help them by not fighting with your spouse in front of them. You can help them by living happily with your better half and children. You can help them by respecting and supporting each other. You can help them leading a happy married life with your spouse and children. You can help them by not getting separated from partner. Separation often results in helplessness, anger, confusion, sadness, guilt, and self-blame. After separation, one may engage in self-blame, and another might turn that lens outwards and blame others. It not only affects you and your spouse but also your parents and children. **Learn the art of adjustment and understand the benefit of compromise. Ego easily destroys relationships no matter how strong the relationship is. So, skip "e" and let it "go". Otherwise, it extinguishes the light of the lamp and can push you to darkness. Neither you win nor your partner, only ego**

wins when you fight with your spouse or loved ones.

Help them creating a pleasant and peaceful atmosphere at home. Prepare good & tasty food for your parents occasionally. Help them by not scolding your children in front of your parents. They feel bad, and it's painful for them to see their grandchildren abused right in front of their eyes. **Allow your kids to be with them and play with them but don't take advantage of their baby-sitting service.** You can help by taking them out for a walk and tell them interesting events, stories, and incidents. Remind them their sacrifice and their importance in your life. Let them tell their past life stories and allow them to share their past challenges and stories.

Help them to be physically solid and mentally strong. Motivate them to do regular walking, exercise, and yoga. Take them to their friends and relatives often. Invite their friends and loved one's home. Get them newspapers, magazines, and books. Bring them what helps and do what enhance their health and happiness.

Don't just be physically present in the house playing a computer game, watching TV, or using a mobile phone, but talk to them; Don't always be busy working on a laptop, but spend some time with them. Play with them, joke with them and read a book out loud for them. Go outside together, take them for a walk and share your new learnings. Ask them about their struggling days and learn how they handled their difficult situations. Question them on their life experience and talk to them about their childhood.

Spend quality time with them. **Plant positive thoughts in their mind.** Small things such as a warm hug, a joke, an appreciation, a recognition, a thank, a salute, a kiss on their cheeks, and just a touch can boost their energy and happiness. It's important to show that you care for them, and you love them. It gives them power.

Your success matters. And it matters a lot to them. So, help them through your grand success. And make them happy though your achievements. **But let there be humility, politeness, and gentleness even in success. Be successful, help others to succeeded.**

Your help helps you! Yes. It's true that your help helps you back. To understand and experience the same, you can just help someone in need and see how you feel after helping them. Solace someone and see what you feel like. Soothe someone and see the change in you. Comfort someone and see how you feel. Make someone happy and watch what happens within you. **Basically, by doing good, you feel good.** So, if helping someone can make us happy, then imagine how much happiness it can give you when you help your own parents. Their good wishes would certainly help you, and their blessings would surely protect you.

Don't you feel happy after helping your parents? Don't you feel relaxed after serving other? Don't you feel contented relieving others from pain? Yes. It brings the feel of satisfaction within you, and you feel delighted after helping others. This feeling of self-satisfaction not only makes you feel good and pleasant but also make others happy.

When you help your parents, they feel happy. They feel proud. They feel contented. They get pleased. They get new energy. They feel comfortable. They feel recognized. They believe you. They understand your love. They experience satisfaction. They feel honoured. They get delighted. The mind gets pacified. They experience the feeling of reward. It's a feeling of self-satisfaction. They feel pleasant. They feel respected. They enjoy the feeling of admiration. They feel revered. Positivity runs in their blood and brings positive feelings into their hearts.

Don't you feel guilty if you don't help them when they look at you for your help? It's okey if you don't help when they don't expect it. It's okey if you do not help when they don't need it. Its okey if you can't help when they can manage themselves, but you must help them when they expect your help during their difficult times; you must help them in their old age and must help them when all their doors are closed. Don't mention your difficulties, inabilities and helplessness but get ready to cross your limitations.

Parents may become a burden to their children at one point of time. When parents get old, they stop earning; they stop working, and they stop helping. They become dependent on children for their daily needs and necessities. This is when parents start looking like irritants. Grown-up sons and daughters start realising that their parents are short tempered, they always fall sick; their medical treatment is expensive; they are too talkative; they don't listen to what is said; they do not let us do what we want to do; there is no privacy, and their presence not gives freedom. Bringing their friends home may become embarrassing for children. Going on a holiday vacation becomes challenging for them. But don't forget that they also have gone through same and similar situations because of you. Even they have forgone their outings and vacations for you; even they have given up their carrier and aspirations for you. And even they have scarified their freedom and privacy for your sake.

If you can tolerate your children and spouse at home, why can't your parents? If you can accept all the inconveniences caused by your children, then why can't parents? If you can tolerate the annoyance of your children and spouse, then how come it becomes so difficult to tolerate your parents? If you can endure the frustration caused by your spouse, then why does it become so difficult to endure the frustration caused by your parents? If you can handle the angriness, sickness, issues, concerns, and challenges of your children and spouse, then why can't you handle your parents'? It's not only your responsibility but also a duty to ensure that your elderly parents are comfortable and well taken care of.

Use your heart to judge your parents rather brain. Use your emotions to understand them rather knowledge. Attach your emotions when you are working for them. Be mentally prepared to help them wholeheartedly when they need your service. Have a better plan to handle the situation when they depend on you for their day-to-day activities, buy necessary machines and tools to take care of them when they are bedridden. Remember, whether it's your father or mother, you will never get another. After all, what they need in their old age is your love, care, patience, and a little place in your heart.

Promise to forgive their mistakes if any. Don't punish them forever for the same. Remind yourself that parents are also human beings. They may have handled many situations for the first time in life. After all, they are not trained and experienced professional parents. They learned the art of parenting with time and age. The best thing that we can do about their mistakes is to forget and forgive. If possible, learn from your parents' mistakes and try to be a better parent but forgive them for their mistakes.

In most of the cases, mistakes happen but are not intentionally made. The important question here is: "**What is more important, the person or their mistakes?**" If you think the person is important, then you should ignore the mistake. If you think the mistake is important, then ignore the person. To be happier in life, we must learn to accept a person along with their mistakes. There is no choice here. Because the perfect person is not born yet. **When we realize that the person is more important than their troubles and mistakes, relationship will survive.**

What do you do when your children make mistakes? We teach them, we try to educate them, we try to explain them, we try to coach them and try to train them. Of course, it is difficult and different with elderly parents, but remember that **parents become children after crossing a certain age.** It may be difficult to handle the situation, but one must mentally be prepared well in advance to manage it better.

Can a small child talk clearly? The same thing happens when parents get too old. Can a child walk properly? The same thing happens when parents get older. Can a child eat properly? The same thing happens to parents when they get old. Can a child sit properly? The same thing happens to parents when they get old. Can a child walk without support? Same with parents. Does your child understand properly when you tell something? It's the same with parents. Does your child listen to you properly? No, you may have to tell them repeatedly. The same thing happens with parents. Can your child take care of itself? Can your child prepare its own food? Similarly, parents. Can your child drink the water properly without spilling it? Does your child often fall sick? Do you need to drop your child off at school? Do you need to pick up your child from school? Or have you arranged transport for your child? The same is true for parents, who require drop-off and pick-up services as well as transportation to and from hospitals. Does your child make the same mistakes again and again?

Does your child speak to itself? Does your child get angry at you? Does your child cry? Does your child shout at you? Does your child irritate you? Does your child make you angry? Does your child complain? Does your child fight with you? Does your child listen to everything you say? Can your child take a bath on its own? Do you lose your patience while dealing with our children? But does your child love you unconditionally? So as your parents. Does your child feel bad if you shout at it? Or does it feel left alone if you do not spend time with it? So as your parents...

If parents become children in their old age, then children should become their parents in their young age. Yes. Children should learn the art of becoming parents of their parents in their last stage.Treat your parents the way you would like to be treated by your children and learn to treat your parents the way you treat your children.

.

Please Don't...

.

Please don't feel bad
Now I can't stand
Please hold my hand
Now I can't withstand

.

I helped you eat
When you start eating
I helped you walk
When you start walking

.

I helped you read

When you start reading
I helped you write
When you start writing

.

Please don't feel bad
I am not able to stand
Now, help is my need
Extend your helping hand

.

Don't cheat me
My eyes are already cheating
don't abuse me
My body is already abusing

.

Don't hurt me
My health is doing it
Don't insult me
My age is doing it anyway

.

Please don't feel bad
I am not able to stand
Please don't get upset
The sun of my life is getting set.

.

CHAPTER NINE

HAPPINESS

Your next gift is to promise that "I will keep my parents happy." Happiness is a mental state in which one feels that all is well, and everything is going to be well. Though happiness is ephemeral and temporary like any other human feelings, but one should always try to be calm, stable, satisfied and happy in life. Generally, we think that happiness comes from money. Of course, money is very important. It can solve many of our problems and can give happiness to a great extent, but money is neither the only source nor the permanent source of happiness. The happiness can emanate only from a peaceful mind. A mind can be peaceful only when the sense of contentment or satisfaction is experienced. So, **the eternal source of happiness is in the sense of overall contentment or in the feel of complete satisfaction. But the feel satisfaction can only be experienced when the objectives are fulfilled. So, it is very important to set the right objectives with noble motives and good intentions.**

True that it is difficult to keep ourselves happy all the time. Ture that we ourselves cannot remain happy for a long period of time. If we ourselves find it hard to remain happy for a long period of time, how can we promise to keep others happy? True. Keeping others happy is not an easy task. **Because happiness depends on age, needs, wants and environment which are not fixed but constantly change;** what makes you happy at the age of 5 or 10 may not make you happy at the age of 20 or 30. What keeps you happy in the current environment may not give you pleasure in a new environment. Today's want may not be relevant tomorrow, and today's need may be immaterial tomorrow.

True that it is not so easy to keep someone happy but our parents did their best to understand us, our needs, wants, desires and the environment. They honestly tried to do what was necessary and went beyond their limitations for our wishes and desires. They saw their happiness in our happiness; they got satisfied in our satisfaction, and they found their peace of mind in our peace. They crossed their boundaries for our bliss and tried their best for our happiness.

They did not mind the troubles we gave them; they did not get angry at the inconveniences we caused; they did not get fed up with our irritations and annoyance; They did not murmur and blame the situation. They went a step ahead and put our comfort above theirs. Their children's happiness was their first preference. They kept quite when we suddenly grabbed and ate what they were eating; They were calm when we quickly changed the TV channel that they were interestingly watching, And They did not lose their patience when we kept on irritating them while they were speaking to someone or doing something. **Because our happiness not only lies in our own happiness but also lies in others happiness too. If you want to be happy, learn to keep people around you happy.**

True that they did their best to keep us happy. Right that they went beyond their limitations to fulfil our wants, and we agree that they crossed their boundaries for our happiness. So what? They did it as it was their duty and it was their responsibility. But why should I promise to keep them happy? Is it my duty? Is it my responsibility too?

Instead of thinking, 'Why should I keep my parents happy?" think, 'Why I should not?' Stop reading the book for 5 minutes. Close the book. Close your eyes. Try to find an answer for: "Why I shouldn't keep my parents happy?" Certainly, your mind goes blank. and realise that there are no reasons to not to keep them happy. But there are certainly many reasons to make them happy. **The first and most important reason is to be happier.** Keeping them happy not only gives self-satisfaction but also gives happiness and peace of mind. Keeping them happy is not only your moral responsibility but is also a moral duty. It's a labour of love and a sign of respect. You should keep them happy for your complacency; should keep them happy for self-contentment; should keep them happy for your inner peace and keep them happy for their satisfaction and sacrifice. **Irrespective of whether it's your duty or responsibility, it's an attitude of gratitude.**

If you are a student, you can make them happy by studying well for your own bright future. Look at the double benefits here... By studying well for your own bright future, you can make your parents happy and proud! So, focus on your education. Give your 100% to your studies. You are sent to schools and colleges for your education and for overall personality development to become a better human being. But if you indulge in bad habits, love affairs, and new relationships in your tender age, it hurts them. It injures them. It not only makes them sad but also spoils your future. Do not get into such immoral affairs or unethical relationships at young age or at any point of time.

It could burn you alive and can kill you without taking your life. Just concentrate on your subjects, lessons, sports, and school activities during studies. Do stay away from bad friends and new relationships during your studies. You will certainly get betrayed by such attractions and will get cheated in your innocence. Instead, focus on your goals and its execution.

You can make your parents happy with your character, conduct, and behaviour. Their children's good character and behaviour always make parents happy, and your virtue keep them contented. Never do anything that breaks their trust and never involve in anything that brings bad name to them. **Don't spoil their name and never damage their dignity in the society.**

You can make your parents happy by getting into a good profession, landing in a good job, or start earning money in the right way at the right age. They feel happy to see you earning, they feel proud to see you growing, and they enjoy your success. Share your achievements with them. Be it your promotion, salary hike, capital gain, you are becoming parent, buying a house, owning a car, winning a prize or any good news, etc. They will be the happiest people to know that you are successful and happy.

Understand, value, and respect your parents' opinion and feelings. It makes them happy if you listen to their advice. It makes them happy if you do not get into arguments showing stubbornness. Their pain is in your pain, and their happiness lies in your happiness. So, be happy to make your parents happy. But never make them or anyone sad just to be happy. Be cautious that your joke, talk, or walk should never become a reason for someone's pain. **Other's pain should never bring joy in us.**

Do not let your ego get to you. Once you hit the teen hood, you may start believing that you know better than them; you think that you understand more than them; you feel that you are the best; they are far behind than you; they don't know much; they are not up to date and are not much intelligent. You would start arguing to prove that you are more intelligent than them and you would start claiming that you are better than them. But remember that they are still older than you and much more experienced than you. **Keep in mind that the arguments will never win hearts but worsen the relationship and will weaken the connection.Understand the fact that blood relationships can survive only with tolerance, patience, love, care, and sacrifice.**

You can make your parents happy by getting married at the right age. You can make them happy by respecting their likes, dislikes, wishes, and expectations while choosing your partner. Your parents can never be happy if you are not happy with your spouse and children. Your parents cannot be happy if your married life is not successful. So, you can always give preference to your heart while choosing your life partner, but make sure that your parents are also part of your decision while choosing your partner.

Show your gratitude, Be grateful. Show your thankfulness and be thankful. They have done a lot for you and still doing. You can simply count all the blessings, gains, benefits, helps, and advantages of having parents in your life. Sum it up. Assign the currency value to realise their economic contribution and the profit you made because of their help and support. Show your gratitude by writing a gratitude letter or a thank-you email to them. It can be shown by sending an appreciative SMS or text message also. It can be best expressed through phone calls or appreciating them directly face to face. It boosts their happiness and energy.

Make your father happy to make your mother happy and make your mother happy to make your father happy. Respect your father if you want to see your mother happy. Respect your mother if you want to see your father happy. They would like to see admiration for each other in the eyes of their children. They would like to see the love and respect for their life partner in the eyes of their children. Honour them with your love and respect. They have quarrelled because of you. They have argued with each other because of you. They have fought with each because you, and they also have fought together with others for of you. So, when you are truly sorry, apologize.

You can keep them happy by maintaining a good relationship with your siblings. They want you to love and care your brothers and sisters. They want you to help them when they need your help, and they want you to support them when they need your support. It becomes difficult for parents to be happy when their children are in fight with one another. **One child makes them parents but two make them referee.** It becomes hard for them to be joyful when their children quarrel with each other. In fact, they feel sad and get depressed when they see their own blood at loggerheads. But they enjoy seeing their children love each other. They like to see their children getting along and respecting one another. And they feel proud seeing their children helping one another in their difficult times.

Your parents deserve your respect. Show them the respect and make them feel that they are important to you. Make them feel that they have a significant place in your heart. Do not disrespect and never insult them. If you feel like throwing harsh words, speak to them in private, but not in front of others. **Never show the knowledge of your words and the sharpness of your tongue to those who taught you how to speak.Remember that you can't recover the words after they are said, and you can't lift the tears after they are dropped down.**

You can make your parents happy by providing financial security in their old age. While doing the financial planning for your future needs and requirements, while making investments for your children, while saving money for your spouse, while buying an insurance policy to safeguard your family, do not forget your parents. Provide them with financial protection and take the necessary actions to defend them. Your investment strategy can help them maintain their dignity and self-esteem. It boosts their self-confidence and gives them assurance. It gives courage walk with head held high in the society. So, set up a separate financial plan for their ageing needs and necessities.

Keep yourself fit and healthy to make them happy. Your parents get hurt when they see you unhealthy, unfit, sick, ill, stressed, and weak. It would be a great help to them if you could keep yourself fit, and healthy. Keep your body strong and mind peaceful. Do physical exercise, walk regularly, and eat healthy. **Invest in yourself and make yourself happy.** Avoid junk food, avoid bad people, and take enough rest. Wake up early in the morning and go to bed early in the night. **Stop watching mobile phone overnight!** Do whatever is necessary to keep yourself fit and fine.

Your parents cannot see your death. It hurts them the most. Make sure that you take extreme care of yourself. Protect yourself from bad health, save yourself from bad habits and shield yourself from risky stunts. Protect yourself from bad thoughts and disassociate yourself from bad people. Be safe, be secured, and always be healthy. Be responsible, be dutiful, and follow healthy lifestyle. Be cautious and never put your life in danger for the sake of excitement or for entertainment.

Your parents cannot see you unemployed. It hurts them a lot when they see you doing nothing. So, **never depend on others**. It's painful for every parent to see that their children depending on them or someone even after crossing the age of 25. It's not only a big burden on them but also on you. **Financial independence should be the priority for any self-esteem individual.** Ensure that your life gets settled and you are financially independent before 25. Dependents lose their respect and value. They get disrespected by their own parents, spouse, children, friends, relatives, and society. **So, earn respect, give respect and be respectful.** Be successful and show them your success. Be grateful and show them your greatness. Aim high, do big. Be good and do good.

Studies across the world are revealing that parents are often reluctant and unwilling to say the facts out loud. Studies and surveys conducted across the world reveal that, parents often report statistically significantly lower levels of happiness. The strains associated with parenthood are not only limited to the period during which children are physically and economically dependent but also after that.

Have you ever thought, how many times you might have hurt your parents? how many times you may have annoyed them? How many times you might have irritated them? How many times you may have driven them insane? How many times you may have made them fight with each other? Countless! Yes, you have hurt, annoyed, irritated, saddened, disappointed, troubled, insulted, vexed, bugged, and bothered them many times. They have tolerated it and endured it all for your sake.

It stings them when you say, "Stop it," while they are telling you what they are telling. Don't hurt your parents with your rough words like, "What have you done for me?" or "How much have you made for me?" or "You spoiled my life" or "It's because of you." **Stop saying more than necessary.**

It hurts them when you don't wish them on their birthday. It mildly hurts them when you miss their marriage anniversaries or any important dates of their life. Don't miss to wish them on their Birthdays and don't skip their wedding anniversaries. Celebrate Mother's Day and party for Father's Day. Take them out for a nice lunch or arrange a dinner party. A thank you card or an emotional appreciation from the bottom of your heart makes them happy. If you cannot wish them in person, at least call them, send them flowers or a greeting card on their birthdays and anniversaries.

It's painful to know that their children have gotten married without even bringing it to their attention. It disappoints them when their children marry against their wishes. But it injures when they realise that their own children did not even invite them to their marriage. It kills to know that their own blood betrayed them. And it destroys them mentally when you intentionally cheat them and spoil their reputation in the society.

When you are on the verge of getting married and during the initial days your marriage, show them that their importance is not diminished. Around that time, may feel that you are going away from them or that someone is taking you away from them. Pulse with their feelings and emotions. Enjoy the beginning of your new life but don't disregard them in your enthusiasm and zeal. Don't ignore them in the speed of your joy and excitement.

It hurts your parents when your spouse disrespects them. It hurts when your spouse insults them. It pains when your spouse's relatives neglect them. And it distresses them when you disregard them. Please educate your new spouse to behave respectfully with your parents, and you should also behave respectfully with your spouse's parents. Never disrespect them, never misbehave with them, and never treat them rudely. **You can never keep your spouse happy insulting your partner's parents and you can never be happy ridiculing his or her family members.**

It hurts when you laugh at them on their language and knowledge, it brings in unhappiness when you make fun of their appearance, and mistakes. It wounds when you avoid them, and it irritates when you insult their relatives and friends. So, **accept them as they are, they can't change themselves at that age as per your expectations and needs.**

Relations are important. Have a good relationship with your relatives. Hating or fighting with your kinfolks upset your parents. They do not like to see you fighting with your blood, kins and people around you. Speak to them with love and treat them with respect. If can't treat them properly, avoid them or stay away from them but don't hate and never get into fight. As said, it's better to be alone than in bad company. If you can't love or respect them, just stay neutral.

It hurts them when they see their adult children fighting among themselves for their property; it hurts when they see their children getting separated and hate each other for the same reason. They not only get depressed looking at their children's disagreement, aversion, and jealousy but also suffer looking at their opposition and hatred towards each other. Parents moan when they see their adult children continue their enmity with their brothers and sisters even after the final settlement of their parent's property dispute. They groan when they see the dissatisfaction and hatred in their children's eyes that the other one has been given more, and I have been given less. They wail when their adult children go to the extent of cheating, betraying and killing their own brothers and sisters for their property. But adult children forget that the **wealth obtained through fraud, betrayal and bloodshed will never bring happiness and peace of mind.** In order to avoid such fights between their children, parents try to make a legitimate "will" for easy dispersal of their wealth. But one of the overly intelligent children go to court and prove that their father or mother did not have mental stability while making the "will." They attempt to prove that their parents were nearly insane in their final stage. They win the case in court and get a better share. Without any hesitation or shame, they feel proud that they won the case proving that their parents had gone mad in their last stage. **Instead of fighting for their property, assent and wealth; can we remain their property? Can we try to be an asset to the society, and can we become the wealth of the country?**

What if I am not able to keep them happy? Think, what would you do when you were not able to keep your children happy? Think what your parents would have done if they were in your position. The answer can help you to determine your action in such situation. Try to convince yourself that it is your responsibility to keep them happy. Prove yourself that it is your obligation to make them feel glad. If nothing works, its okey but don't ignore them; don't insult them; don't cheat them, and never betray them. If you can't stretch yourself to keep them happy, its fine but never escape from your basic duty and never run away from your fundamental responsibility. Its okey if you can't comfort them but never discomfort them. Its okey if you can't keep them happy but never make them sad. Its okey if you can't give them the bliss but never bring agony.

Be Happy

Make Your Mother Happy
She prays for you
Make Your Father Happy
He gives his name & blessings to you
Keep Yourself Happy
It gives health, happiness, and prosperity to you

Don't hurt her, and never ignore her
She is your mother
Don't cheat him, and never disrespect him
He is your father
Don't get annoyed, and don't get irritated
When you become their need.

Be a Good Daughter
Make your father Proud and honored
Be a Good Son
Make your mother Proud and delighted
Be a Good human
Make yourself proud and satisfied

Be a good person
Bring your father, the respect

Be a good soul
Show your mother, the love
Be a good individual
Respect the love and life given.

.

CHAPTER TEN

Financial Discipline and Security

If a gift can enhance the financial security of your parents, then why can't it be gifted? Yes. Your 10th gift is to promise that "I obey financial disciplines and build a financially secured life for my parents." Along with your financial stability, their economic security is also your responsibility.

You have been supported. You have been helped and you have been maintained for a long period of time by your parents. Now, it's your turn. When you start earning, ensure that your parents are economically happy and healthy. **Follow the financial rules in your young age and support your parent's financial needs in their old age.** Like how being financially fit is not only your responsibility but also a duty, shielding your parents from economic turmoil is not only your responsibility but also a moral duty.

You may have seen your parents spending their money cautiously. You may have heard them often saying "Don't waste money", "Turn off lights if not needed", "Money doesn't grow on trees", "Keep your belongings responsibly", "It's just a waste of money" or "it's not worth it" Etc., Etc., You may have seen them working overtime.

You may have seen them hopping from one shop to another inquiring about the price of the product that they want to buy. You may have seen them bargaining for the right price, you may have seen them walking to the farthest shop instead of buying from the nearest one. You may have also seen them making investments in real estate, equity market, gold Etc... Why do they do all these things? Because they understand the value of money and the power of investment. **They know that the money they are saving today will make their and their children's life easier tomorrow.**

They chose smaller or medium-sized hotels instead of an expensive one. They look for less costlier restaurants instead of expensive one. You may have seen your dad buying lesser priced shoes, shirts, and other required things when it comes to his needs. Mother settling down with inexpensive outfit, ornaments, and things when it comes to her wants. **They learn the art of getting satisfied with less.** Though they can afford high standard one, they prefer lesser or medium priced. Even if they look miser in the eyes of their own children and niggard from their relatives' point of view, they give up on expensive purchases and say no to a luxury. **Because they know that the money, they are saving today is going save their children tomorrow.**

Have you seen your parents working hard? Have you seen them working extra hours? Have you seen them leave home early to work and coming back late at night? Have you them saving money? Have you seen them working even after their retirement? Have you seen your them working though they have got enough money for their life? Do you know why? **Because they don't want to depend on you and burden you in the coming days.**

Have you seen your parents invest money in financial schemes? Have you seen your parents buying property? Have you seen your parents taking out loans? Have you seen your parents struggling to pay EMI? Have you seen your parents nominating you as nominee for their financial policies? Have you seen your parents buying insurance policies? Have you seen your parents giving you financial knowledge and advice? Have your seen parents saving your money for your own self? Have you seen your parents saving their money for your future? Have you seen them taking extra care of their health in their old age? Do you know why? Because they want to make your life easier, comfortable, stress free along with theirs. They don't want to become a burden on you in their old age. They want you to be relaxed and secured, they want you to be calm and contended and **they want you to lead a blissful life without facing financial hardship and distress.**

Have you seen your parents lead a simple life saving more? Have you noticed your parents sacrificing their wants and wishes? Have you seen them saving money for your marriage? Have you seen them spending their money carefully and cautiously? Have you seen their effort to secure your financial life even after their death? Have you seen them mortgaging their jewellery and valuables for your sake? And have you seen them getting ready to sell their inherited property and hard-earned assets for your sake? Do you know why? What's driving them to do so? It's you & your future. **They want to make your present pleasant and future secure.**

Did they financially support you until you started supporting yourself? Did they provide you with food, clothing, and shelter until you started earning? Did they provide you with education and medical care? Did they fulfil your needs and wants? Did they fulfil most of your demands if not all? If so, what are you doing to make their life easier? Do you have any financial plan in place to support their future? How are you planning to make their present pleasant and future secure? What action items do you have in place to meet their future needs and requirements? **It's a competitive world, need start our preparation early.**

Take your first financial step early in life. As early as possible. Start with savings. Because saving is earning. Understand that **every coin saved equals every coin earned.** Don't spend lavishly until you start earning on your own. Remember that "**only the power of earning can give the power of spending.**" Hence, **save your parents' hard-earned money until you understand the difficulty of earning money.** Don't spend it lavishly on luxurious things; don't waste it on show-offs; and never blow it for exhibition.

Earnings are also important along with savings. "Early start, early success" is the mantra. Believe in yourself and start the process of earning money early in life. Don't expect help from others. It is difficult to find helping hands, but opportunistic minds are waiting for us in every corner. If not big, start something small; if not full time, start with part time job but do something. If you don't want to get into it early in life, its okey but start thinking about it early and act responsibly until then.

We are often asked "What you would like to be when you grow up". We say that I would like to become that, this, or something else. But what are you doing now to become that, this, or something else is very important for your success. Don't waste time thinking that I have enough time; I am too young to start now or it is not the right time. Instead, start your preparation now no matter when your exams are; no matter how young or old you are and it doesn't matter if time is right or not. **Do what you can do today to achieve tomorrow's goal. Today's contribution and preparation plays a significant role in your future success. Early preparation and current contributions are the most important actions for your success.** So, swing into action right away and start your preparation now. **'Now' is always the right time to start something good.**

Now a days, everyone is after money, and it is essential too. In today's commercial world, only those who are financially stable and secure can live a respectable life in the society. Money is very important to lead a dignified life. Of course, money is not everything, but it is the most important thing. Of course, money is not everything, but everything needs money. Of course, money can't get you everything, but it can get many things. **The irony is that those who have enough money, think that it is not everything, but those who do not have it, know that it is all and everything.** Even though we want more and run after money, never cheat others for that sake, and never covet another's money or property to accumulate more. Always earn it honestly. In the speed of earning more, don't cheat, don't hurt, and never covet what belongs to others. Make a wage than coveting other's money.

Since it is believed that hard work gets us more money, most of us are busy doing hard work to earn more. In fact, all of us are not just running after money but running after 'more'. People have gone to the extent of lying, misleading, cheating, deceiving, and even killing one another for more money, but are utterly failing to understand what 'more' is, how much 'more' is more and how much is too much! Though we do not know how much we want, we all very well know we want more! Hence, most of us are sincerely putting forth effort to earn more. And many of us are honestly putting in extra effort to earn dishonestly. By the way, how are you earning your money? Honestly or dishonestly? If dishonestly, stop it and start earning honestly.

In fact, life becomes easy when we understand what we want and how much we want! But people are busy earning more without knowing what exactly we want and how much more we need; looks like everyone seems to be busy earning more. It is believed that, only 'more' can help us and save us. Of course, it is difficult to decide how much is too much. Certainly, it is not an easy task. It may be the most difficult calculation of your life. But those who got the formula of this calculation are living happily without much stress and anxiety in life.

In fact, Life demands less from us, but we want more from it. There's nothing wrong in expecting more out of our life. But we should know what to expect, when to expect and how much to expect. To be honest, life is simple, but our wants have made it complicated. If you can control your wants, you can lead a financially happy life. and if you have good goals in life, it will drive you towards happiness & richness. **In fact, life is not difficult, but our egos, desires and expectations have made it horrible.**

Another simple calculation to lead an easy and happy life is to understand the difference between your needs and wants. Life becomes easy and stress-free when you lead a need-based life, but it can get stressful and horrible when it is driven by our wants and desires. So, the awareness, acceptance, and observance of such a need-based simple life can keep us happy and can give us peace of mind. Whereas our unnecessary wants and uncontrollable desires make our mind malicious and stimulate to run behind "more". So, don't let your mind run like a mad horse after every want and desire. Tie it up, control it and tame. Otherwise, **therestless mind will never let you to be happy.**

One another simple rule to lead a peaceful and secured life is to stop comparing yourself with the people around you in terms of clothes, ornaments, money, houses, properties, vehicles, and other materials that we own. Originally, human beings are satisfied animals, but comparison has made them crave for more. Humans are naturally happy animals who become unhappy when they see others experiencing greater happiness. However, if you really want to compare yourself with others, then do it in terms of knowledge, health, kindness, charity, compassion, and contribution to the society.

Of course, we need money, and it must be earned, but we must ensure that it is earned in the right way. While earning money, your focus should not only be on how much is being earned but should also be on how it is being earned. Work hard to earn and work honestly to make it. Honesty may not get you a lot of money all of a sudden but will get you more than that gradually along with good name and respect.

How much being earned is important too, but how your earnings are being handled is more important. Are you earning in one hand and spending in the other? or saving too? Are you investing or not? Do you have a financial goal in life or not? How have you planned to manage your future expenses? As soon as we start earning, we should start saving. **Ensure that the importance is given to savings as well along with your present pleasure.** Earnings without savings is zero. Your savings not only save you but also serve you. Savings not only shows you a way out of worries and uncertainties but also provides you an opportunity to enjoy your life. Your savings not only work for you but also earn for you. So, always respect the money. And **be wise, moneywise.**

If you can work for your children and spouse, if you can plan for your children, and their future needs and requirements, why not parents? Have a financial plan in place and reserve some portion of your savings to manage their old age expenses, medical treatments, trips, and tours.

A mother never works only for herself, and a father never earns only for himself. They work less for themselves and more for their family. In the same way, don't just work to earn for yourself, your spouse, and your children; also, do it for your parents. Give preference to your parents, along with your children and spouse. Reserve a portion of your income for your parents too. We may have heard that "a child comes with a lot of responsibilities." In the same way, we also have responsibilities toward our parents. Strive for their better future along with yours. Plan well in advance to cover all the needs and necessities of the rest of their life. So, don't just make more money, learn to spend for noble causes too. So, don't just concentrate on making more money, but also learn to spend it on your parents too.

- Make some investment in the equity market for your parents.
- Buy real estate for them.
- Gift them gold and diamond jewellery.
- Buy an insurance plan and save some money for their future.
- Deposit money in their name.

- Buy some mutual funds or do a systematic investment plan.
- Reserve cash for their emergency

And be the nominee of all your above investments. With this strategy, you can secure your parents' life as well as your own. The return on your investments is going to return to you when it gets matured. It gives them the feeling of safety, and at the same time, it gives you the confidence to manage any unforeseen risks, unexpected expenses, and emergency situations.

If you can plan ahead of time for your children's education and marriage, why can't you plan ahead of time for your parents' old age expenses? The first thing that you need to do is to accept their responsibility. When the responsibility is accepted, the path becomes clear, and opportunity opens up to save more for them.

So then, how much should I save or reserve for my parents' needs and expenses? Maybe up to 20-25% of your savings can be reserved for your parents' needs and necessities. 40-50% for yourself and your spouse and divide the remaining 40-25% between your children, and the nation.

Do you know if your parents have enough earnings or savings to manage their left-out life? Do you know how are they going to manage their elderly expenses? Are they financially secured for the rest of their life? If they have not set aside any money or property for themselves, then take accountability of creating assets for them. take responsibility of managing their expenses. They must have forgotten being busy in your upbringing or they may have spent it all managing family expenses. **Don't just fly away getting married and don't just run away sucking**

everything they had. Take their responsibility too.

When we start earning money, our roles and responsibilities change; eventually it gets exchanged in the family. Life becomes not only interesting but also challenging when roles begin to change and exchange. Till now, you were thinking about how to spend money, but now you will start thinking about how to save money. Up until now, you were being taken care of by your parents, but now you are the caretaker. Till now, you were expecting your parents to do something for you, now you are expected to do what is needed for them. So far, you were dependent on them, but now they may become your dependents. Until now, you were their responsibility, but now they are your responsibility. So, open your umbrella wide open and include them along with you.

Understand their wish list. What do they want to do? Where do they want to go? What do they want to see? What do they want to learn? Whom do they want to meet? How do they want to live? When do they want to do what? Assist them in doing what they want to do, seeing what they want to see, and take them where they want to go. Reserve some space for their expenses in your financial planning.

Providing them with financial security during their old age is one of the greatest services that one can offer to their parents. The financial security not only gives them mental peace but also gives them emotional safety.

But what can I do if I am not able to support them in their ripe old age? What shall I do if I am not able to help them in their difficult time? Think.... Ask yourself what would you do when you were not able to help your children in their critical time? And think what your parents would have done if they were in your position. The answer will direct your actions and can drive you out from such situations. But don't slowly slip away from your responsibilities.

Instead of taking on their parents' responsibilities, few adults become burden to them. In some cases, they become a curse of their parents' life. How about you? Are you hurting them? Are you putting pressure on them with your wants and demands? Are your expectations and expenses spoiling their peace of mind? Do you just submit your wish list to them and wait for fulfilment? Are you straining them with your unlimited wants and wishes? Are you putting them through emotional turmoil? Is your young age and youthfulness ruining their old age? Is your peer pressure making their life miserable? Is your existence causing them problems? Is your behaviour brining tears from their eyes? **Are you their curse or boon?** It's ok if you can't secure their future, but don't spoil. It's fine if you can't provide the financial security, but don't jeopardise their happiness in the winter of their life and don't spoil the existing peace of their mind in the evening of their life. Just do what is essential.

Money My Darling.

Money, you are the honey
You make us strong
You make us weak
You make us Boney and also, Bonny

Money, you are the honey
You make us rich
You make us poor
You make us big and also, small

.

Money, you are the honey
You are the god
You are the ghost
You show the heaven and also, the hell

.

Money, you are the honey
You give the pleasure
And also, the pressure
You give us the life and also, the death

.

Money, you are the honey
Please stay with me
I earn you honestly
Please be with me, I spend you carefully

.

Money, you are the honey
Please be with me,
I respect your presence
Do stay with me, I know the value of your absence

.

CHAPTER ELEVEN

Final Responsibility

The eleventh gift is all about being with your parents and living along with them. Stay with them in the evening of their life and be with them till the end of their life. **Don't leave them, live with them.**

Children think that their parents are great, very loving, very caring, very kind, nice, benevolent, protective, and are super when they are around 5 years of age. At 10, they think that their parents are good, they know everything, they are funny, they are strong, they are helpful, they are kind-hearted, selfless, soft-hearted and are their role models. At 15, their parents are nice but short-tempered; they impose so many conditions on everything; they do not understand children; they do not allow us to be free; they are sceptics, whereas their friends' parents are very good. When children are around 20, they feel that their parents are outdated, they do not understand anything, they put a lot of restrictions on them, they inquire a lot, and they ask too many questions. They do not grant freedom. They try to control our life. Not letting us to lead our life the way I want. At 25, they feel that parents raise objections to everything, they interfere, and intervene in our personal lives. They are judgemental, they don't let us make our own decisions; they put us under pressure and criticize a lot.

At or around 30, children have become parents, and they think that it's difficult to manage our children; life is not easy, and children are very fast, sensitive, and expensive. Our parents did so much for us at 40; they sacrificed a lot for us; they faced so many difficulties and challenges; how did they manage it all? They have a lot of patience, they are very disciplined, and they are strong. At 50, they did a lot for us; I wonder how they managed everything; they were great!

It takes 40-50 years for children to understand that parents are great, what they felt when they were at 5. It takes almost half a century to realize the importance, significance, sacrifice and value of their parents. What about you? Do you also take 50 years to understand and realize their greatness?

While living with the people, misunderstandings, misconceptions, troubles, and quarrels are common; problems bother, and ego disturbs. Even then, we continue to live with them and they continue to live with us. It doesn't mean that they are perfect or we are perfect, but we accept their imperfection and they accept our imperfection. Otherwise, it's difficult to live together.

Your parents question you when you appear to be on the wrong path. They scold you when you are not doing the things right. They correct you when you are incorrect. They teach you when you don't understand. They criticize you to correct, they assess to guide, and they identify the faults to fix the problems in you. They advise you for your benefit, and counsel you for your profit. But your immature half-baked mind may not take it positively and your ego may not let you listen to them. If you don't want them to correct you, then who should? As a parent, they scold you; they question you, and they correct you. As a parent, they assess you, comment on you and find fault in you to fix it. Don't get irritated when they ask you to take responsibility and remind you of your duty. Don't get upset when they don't allow you to do whatever you would like to do; don't get annoyed when they advise you; don't get angry and don't get emotional when they prepare you for the real world. **Its foolishness to get upset, just because they try to correct your mistakes.**

You need to understand that they are preparing you to face the real challenges of life; they want you to face the world fearlessly without running away from problems; they want you to lead your life in the right direction; They want you to be successful so that you can stay happy. They want you to be flawless; they want you to be dutiful; they want you to do better, and they want you to understand the value of your life. Afterall, what they want? They want you to be more responsible, successful, and dutiful; so that you can lead a peaceful and blissful life.

They selflessly do their duty throughout their life. They spend the prime time of their life to help you become an independent and self-dependent. Now it's your time. If they need your help to stand on their own legs, ensure that you are there. Don't show your gratitude just by making phone calls, visiting them occasionally, or sending some money; but be there next to them, standing firm to do what is necessary. Parents usually are not demanding, but that does not mean they should not be given. Be a giver than a receiver in life.

Your parents ensured food, safety, clothing, and education until you stood on your own. Now, if they can't stand on their own legs, ensure that they get good food, care, and a better life. It's your turn to give back. Don't just move on without considering their needs and emotions.

Don't just escape without making the necessary arrangements. Isn't it true that they spent around half of their life taking care of you, your needs, wants, requirements, and wishes? If so, why can't you get prepared to take care of their sinking life?

It is okey to be away but get back to them when needed. They will be in need of physical support when they get older. Minimum support is required during their 60s. medium support in their 70s, and maximum support is to be provided during their 80s and onwards. In fact, parents may start behaving like children at the end of their 70s but become children in their 80s. Yes. Human body starts behaving differently after 50, slows down after 60; and starts shutting down after 70. A day after 80 is a bonus these days. So, mentally be prepared to treat them like children and be physically ready to handle them like kids. They need childlike care in their second childhood because man loses control over senses and become dependent on others in dotage.**Human life starts out as a dependent and ends-up as a dependent.**

They will not have enough strength in their body; they will not have power in their arms, and they will not have enough vision in their eyes. They may behave silly. and may act like a child. Like how a small child cries when something is denied; like how a small child falls while walking; like how a small child throws when it does not like something; like how a small child drops while eating; like how a small child spills while drinking; like how a small child cries when scared; like how a small child does not care about anyone, and like how a small child speaks its mind. They lose their control over their body and their mind spin out of their control. They become helpless, their strength diminishes, and their power shrinks. Time defeats them and they get wounded by their age. They get frustrated, they feel sad, they murmur, they cry, and complain. They look ugly, they act strange, and they become expensive. Though they are embarrassed by their own act and conduct, things are out of theircontrol. They may bother you; they may insult you; they may irritate you and they may trouble you. But things are out of their reach. They make desperate attempts to overcome their weakness. But fail in front of the time & get defeated by their own age. So, treat them with respect and care. After a stage, their childhood returns, and they behave childish. Remember that your old parents become new children.

They start losing their own support as time goes by; their energy level comes down, confidence level decreases, and their memory starts fading. The power of endurance reduces, and the power of tolerance diminishes. They forget things. Their hands shake. their legs stumble. Fingers tremble. TV irritates. Phone calls bother. Lips lisp. May repeat the same thing again and again and may convey the same message all the time. But don't lose your patience in such conditions and don't get upset in such situations. Understand that it is nature's game, and everyone must go through the same situation. Those who helped us throughout their life need our help now. Those who supported us throughout our life need our support now. **Today it may be your parents who are looking for support, but tomorrow it's going to be you who need it the most!** Especially when our elderly parents become young children, they may need more of our care and absolute support.

They may need your support to eat; they may need your help to drink; they may need your assistance to walk and even to take a bath. And may need to carry them in your hands from one room to another. Their ears are not able to hear, their eyes are not able to see, their hands are not able to work, and their legs are not able to withstand the weight of their own body. They are not able to walk in the direction that they would like to. They are not able to move the way they want to. Organs of their body are not listening to them. Their own body is rejecting their orders and are in agitation against them. The body that supported them throughout their life is conspiring against them, and the mind that helped them throughout their life is deceiving. **Their mind and body are at loggerheads and are fighting like enemies.** There is no coordination between their mind and body, and there is no cooperation among themselves. They are neither in a position to direct their body nor able to control their mind.

Now a days, it's all about me!! My education, my career, my comfort, and my future; my growth; my spouse; my children; my wish; and my will. It's all about me and only about me. There's nothing wrong with taking care of ourselves. But in the name of "I," "You" (others) should not get invisible. Don't forget that they brought us up following "not me, but you" policy but few grown-ups behave like **"it's me or thee"** and they take **"My way or highway"** route. Never forget their care and never ignore their existence while they are alive. Remember that their physical, emotional, and economical safety is your responsibility in their senility.

In this era of globalization and urbanization, the changing lifestyle has made everyone desperate for money. Everyone is running behind it and busy huddling around it. It is clear that most of us are earning for our wants rather than needs. It's good to earn more! But do we know how much is more? How much more is more? And how much more do we want? [Wait, stop reading. Please close the book, close your eyes, and contemplate these questions. Get the answer from your inner soul before you proceed to complete the book] All of us think that 'more' is the new less **and 'more' is the new 'need'. But we are failing to understand that we are not just running behind 'more' but flying behind 'more than others''.** Don't get greedy by looking at what others have; instead, focus on fulfilling your own needs and wants. Don't buy things just because someone else has bought and don't do things just because other have done something. If so, shouldn't we go after money? Then, why is everyone so invested in money? Who will give me the money if I need it? Is money not important? Of course, it is important, and it is very important. But is it more important than your self-respect, strain, tension, stress, happiness, and relationships? Less money is sufficient for need-based life but more is required for want-based life.

As soon as your education is complete, you shift to nearby cities in search of a job. After a few days of struggle in the new city, we may get a good job of our choice and will start earning money. What next? go to the office on time, work overtime to prove that you are the best in your office or business, come home late at night, sleep, get up, get ready, go to work, and try to prove that you are the best. Come back home late at night, sleep, get up, get ready, go to work, and try to prove that you are the best in what you do. Come back home late at night, sleep, get up, get ready.... And it continues for ever.

But what do we do after our "life is financially settled"? Few will get busy with spending, and few focuses on saving. They start building wealth for themselves, their spouse, and their children! How about you? Do you spend your time and money on the needs and comforts of your parents too?

We know that abuse against senior citizens is on the rise all over the world. Fraud, violence, and criminal activity against elderly parents are also on the rise. Senior citizens are being victimised because they are considered a soft target. Seniors are suffering from physical, emotional, and financial abuse. They are duped not only by their own children or caregivers, but also by strangers and others who have gained their trust. By the way, are you trustworthy?

Many of earning children get satisfied by sending money to their parents as and when requested or monthly. If your parents wanted monthly returns, then they could have invested their money in some savings schemes, mutual funds, and fixed deposits to get monthly returns. But they spent their hard-earned money and time growing you up. They spent it on building your future! Don't just get your hands washed by sending some money. Pulsate to their needs and necessities. Remember that your parents need more of your presence than your presents. **Don't leave them at the mercy of their neighbours and relatives. Be with them or keep them with you in their last breath.**

Understand that those who are in the winter of their life, they need help. Old age feebleness takes away their financial independence, strength, and power. Declining years vanishes their beauty, wealth, and health. Time takes away their memories, friends, relatives, and loved ones. And it kills their interest and independence. At the same time, ageing gifts them illness, weakness, loneliness, loss of vision, dependency, deteriorating health, back pain, joint pain, body aches, a fluctuating mind, depression, and many more unwanted favours. Put yourself in their shoes and try to imagine yourself in that situation when such unpleasant, and traumatic situations are imposed on you and such unwelcome favours and gifts are bestowed upon you.

Who is there to get them a tablet when their head is aching? Who will give them a glass of water when they are thirsty at midnight? Who will prepare them lunch and dinner when they feel hungry? Who can bring something to eat when their mouth dries at an odd time? Who will take them to doctor if not well? Who will bring home their daily needs? Who do they talk to? Whom should they share their feelings with? What should they do if sitting at home alone is boring... [Please pause for a moment. Close the book, imagine the situation associated with these questions or subject. Get the answer from your heart before you proceed]

When you feel that they have become a burden on you, if you think that it is difficult to bear their burden, then you should ask yourself three simple questions!

1. How do you want to be treated by your children (in your old age) when you are going to be dependent on them like your parents?
2. How your parents treated you when you were dependent on them?
3. How your parents would have treated you if you were in their place?

You may think that I don't need to be with them just to take care of them. Mother can take care of father. Father can take care of mother, and moreover, relatives are nearby. But, not sure how much relatives can help our parents when we ourselves are so busy somewhere else. But, what to do? We all have obligations in life, such as paying rent, phone bills, children's school fees, house EMI, car loan, and so on. The pragmatic truth is that **"life looks dangerous when there is no money in the pocket."** The true colour of life can be seen only when our pockets are empty. Believe it or not, life will show all seven colours of the rainbow when the balance in your bank account is zero.

So, what should I do now? Should I leave everything and go back to stay with my parents or should continue to do what I am doing? or should I call them to stay with me? What should I do if they do not want to be with me? What shall I do if they are not happy staying with me and my spouse? The answer is simple. Take them into consideration. Get together. Ask them. Discuss and choose the best option works for all. Accordingly, make a collective decision.

It's okey if they are healthy, it's okey if they can manage themselves, it's okey if they do not need anybody's help or support to lead their life. It's ok if they are safe and feel protected wherever they are. Its okey if they are happy and emotionally not dependent on anyone, it's okey if they are comfortable and would like to lead an independent life. But the moment you feel that they are adversely affected by their loneliness and need help, please rush to take care of them without thinking twice about it. Live with them before they leave you. Support them, assist them, and serve them instead of regretting later. It makes no sense to regret seeing their empty chair and vacant beds later. It hurts when grown children ignore their parents. The feeling of abandonment not only strains their heart and intestine but kills them alive.

If you are already living with them and taking care of their needs and necessities, then do it with respect, civility, manners, love, concern, and courtesy. Don't frustrate them to say, 'When are you going away from us?' and don't irritate them to ask, "Leave us alone!" It is easy to get upset. It is easy to get irritated and is easy to get frustrated though you love them. You may feel like yelling at them in anger and screaming at them out of frustration at times. But have patience and maintain your dignity along with theirs. **If you can't curb what's happening, control your emotions and actions.**

Do you remember saying...

"You have already told me 100 times."

"How many times do I have to tell you this?"

"I have already told you many times." Or "Why can't you remember it?"

"You will never change."

If so, please avoid it going forward. It easily hurts anyone when repeated.

The best way to cope with your frustration is to empathise with your parents as they are going through a series of serious problems one after the other, such as dependency, loss of energy, loss of job, loss of independence, loss of their relatives and loss of friends, loss of vision, hearing loss, loss of respect, loss of dignity, loss of control over their emotions, loss of control over their tongue, loss of power, loss of control over their body and loss of control on their own mind, and loss of most everything that you have now. So, avoid using harsh words; they are lethal. **Remember that the higher you move in consciousness, lesser the faults you find in others.**

Don't become a curse on your parents' life. Never make them suffer and struggle in their dotage. If you are one of those kids, it's okey to stay away but don't hurt them in their senility being with them. Don't pressurise them in their advanced age, and don't make their life miserable staying along with them. In some parts of the world, it may be an embarrassing situation for adult children to live with their parents after the age 20–25. Irrespective of your culture, religion, region, comfort, and advantages, do stay with them if they expect you to be around them in their ripe old age. Irrespective of your likes and preferences, you should follow humanity and must discharge your moral duties towards them.

·

After certain time...

After certain time, it's all pain
You like it or not, after certain time
there is no gain, it's all pain

·

Pain becomes partner, burden becomes brother
Sorrow becomes sister, mourn becomes mother
And failure becomes father

·

After certain time, it's all pain
You want it or not, after certain time
there is no gain, it's all pain

·

Fatigue becomes friend, regret becomes relative
Doubt becomes daughter, pleasure becomes stranger
And health becomes an outsider

·

After certain time, it's all pain
You need it or not, after certain time
there is no gain, it's all pain

When their body starts bothering
When their mind starts minding
Be the hope, be their supporting rope

When their leg stops walking
When their hand stops working
Be the support, be their choice by default

When their ears stop listening
When their eyes stop seeing
Be the sense, be their sensory organs

When their pockets are empty
When their cloths get dirty
Be the help, be their helping hand

Because, after certain time, it's all pain
You need it or not, after certain time
there is no gain, it's all pain

When everything is lost
When nothing is left
Be the best, give your shoulder for their rest.

Because, after certain time, it's all pain
You want it or not, after certain time
there is no gain, it's all pain

WHO?

Who, who is that,
Who works harder for you?
Who works longer for you?
Who forgets his lunch
and dinner for you?

.

Who, who is that,
Who builds house for you?
Who grosses money for you?
Who makes his hands dirty
and builds property for you?

.

Who, who is that,
Who earns for you?
Who stands for you?
Who withstands for you
Just for you and only for you?

.

Who, who is that,
Who crosses limits for you?
Who overcommits for you?
Who makes your future liter
And more brighter for you?

.

Contact

Contact
Veerkumar Sondur
+ 91 9611256828

www.ingramcontent.com/pod-product-compliance
Lightning Source LLC
Chambersburg PA
CBHW021405150726
47989CB00005B/2414